The Butterfly Effect

by

Julie McLaren

Copyright © Julie McLaren 2014
All Rights Reserved

No part of this book may be reproduced in any form, by photocopying or by any electronic or mechanical means, including information storage or retrieval systems, without permission in writing from the copyright owner of this book.

With thanks to all the friends and family who have read this novel in various stages of its development and have offered support, ideas and encouragement; also to my sister, Ginny Constable, for the cover design. Thanks also to Kath Middleton for beta reading and other members of the KUF authors' forum for many different forms of advice.

The Butterfly Effect, first proposed by Edward Lorenz in 1972, illustrates vividly one of the central ideas of Chaos Theory. It suggests that, contrary to expectations, small changes in initial circumstances can have major effects on large and complex systems such as the weather. In theory, the beating of a butterfly's wings in one part of the world could affect the intensity of a tornado in another.

December 22nd

It's not a bad room. If you paid fifty quid for something like this, somewhere not that smart or maybe out of season, you wouldn't feel cheated. It's clean, the bed is soft enough and the sheets smell fresh. There's a little desk or dressing table and a chair, and there's carpet on the floor. In one corner there's a door that leads to the smallest en suite you ever saw, but the toilet flushes and the water in the basin is warm. Nothing to complain about, but that's where the similarity to a budget room in a small, slightly run-down hotel ends, and now, to keep myself calm, I'm going to list the things that are wrong. The things that struck me after I'd been awake for a few minutes. The things that made my heart beat hard. Harder. Like a 'spot the difference' competition in a children's comic, I will mentally circle them in turn.

Firstly, the windows are locked and frosted, both in here and in the bathroom. There's a tiny area where the handle used to be, where the frosting is a little worn, and if you put your face right up close you can see the vague outlines of rooftops like an unfamiliar city on a foggy day, but this room could be anywhere. Then there is the huge fridge-freezer in the corner, a monstrous piece of ancient kitchen technology that shudders intermittently and makes a strange roaring sound, like an approaching train at an underground station. Both the fridge and freezer are packed with food, mostly ready meals and frozen produce, but there are a few salad things in the crisper. There's a microwave on the bedside table beside it, with crockery and some packets in the cupboard below, except it's not crockery, it's all plastic, as is the cutlery.Then there is the wardrobe. It has shelves and drawers on one side and a hanging space on the other, with spare bedding and pillows in the long shelf that runs along the top. Nothing strange about that, but it is full of clothes and, unless I'm going completely mad or have amnesia, they are not mine and I didn't put them there. They are my size, and they are uncannily similar to clothes that I possess, but they are all brand new, I can tell. And I would never have organised my things this way; the bras are in with the pants, which is just wrong, and the jumpers are on hangers. It is all nearly familiar but not quite right.

There's one more thing. It's obviously the most important, and I left it until the end in the forlorn hope that it might turn out not to be true, but of course it is. I just went and checked again, to be sure. The door is locked and there is no key. It's not one of those hotel-type locks, not even a Yale. It's just an ordinary mortice lock, but it's strong enough to keep this door firmly closed, and no amount of shaking or kicking makes any difference. I've tried that. Oh yes. And hammering on the wood until my hands ache, and shouting, and yelling, and crying and calling for help, cheek against the door, wet with tears. None of it makes any difference. I don't think there is anyone else in the building; nobody to hear, nobody to help.

That was all some time ago – I don't know how long as my watch has gone – but you can only be like that for so long. Even if nothing has changed, which it hasn't, you can't go on at that pitch for ever. It feels as if your batteries are running out, and then you get an empty feeling and an overwhelming weakness and you can't even cry properly. That's probably why I'm so calm now, why I can conduct this mental inventory in such a dispassionate way, but I've no idea how long it will last. Will I be back on my feet in an hour or so, prowling around like a caged tiger, searching for something that could get me out even though I know there will be nothing? If he's clever enough to have done this, after all this time and all the measures we put in place to stop him – well, he won't have left a key lying around, will he?

The funny thing is, this is actually all my fault. If only

I'd listened to Nat, I would still be safely tucked away where nobody could get to me, but what sort of life is that? I said it to Nat, one evening when he came round to check up on me, that maybe it was time to reduce some of the more extreme measures, take a few more risks, see what would happen, but he was so adamant, so sure that the danger was still there, that I let it drop. I didn't want to worry him any more than was necessary, but the germ of the idea was there and it wouldn't go away. There had to be an alternative to this. There had to be a chance that, one day, I would be able to lead a normal life, to wake up in the morning and go to work and do the things I used to do before this all started. And if that did happen, then it would all be down to Nat, of course it would, but maybe he was just a bit too cautious.

Oh, Nat! That's made me cry all over again! Whatever will he be thinking? He'll blame himself, I know he will. Even though nobody could have done more than he did to keep me safe, he will still feel that he's failed; but it's not his fault that I put myself at risk. I have shed some tears for the other people who may be worrying about me – especially Mum and Dad – but it's Nat I really worry about. The best friend anyone could ever have, and there's nothing I can do to make it any better for him, to let him know that I'm still alive, at the moment, anyway.

That has also made me realise how my life has shrunk since this all started. If this had happened, if I had suddenly disappeared two years ago, there would have been dozens of people wondering what had happened to me, texting each other, posting things on Facebook, starting some kind of campaign to find me. Olga and the others in the band, all the people at school, most of my uni friends, they have all been whittled away as my means of communication have been reduced and I have spent less and less time out of the house. Now they will only find out when they see it on the television. Victim of stalking abducted. At least they will know that we were right though, that we weren't being paranoid. At least there is that.

Two years ago. It's hard to believe that so much can happen in such a relatively short time and that my life could be changed quite so radically. I'd have laughed if you'd told me then, as I rushed home from work to prepare for the gig, butterflies of excitement and fear in my stomach, that the road I was taking would lead me here, to this room. I might have laughed, but would I have taken it seriously enough to have changed out of my sparkly top and phoned Olga? Sorry, Olga, but I don't think I want to sing in a band after all. She would have been a bit cross, we may even have fallen out, but I wouldn't be here now.

But then, maybe Richie and I would never have got together. Maybe we wouldn't have had that blissful time together. I may never have known what it is to find someone who totally gets you, understands what you're thinking before you've even registered the thought. Someone who loves you exactly as you are. Even though I lost him, I don't think I could choose a path that didn't include him, so if Richie and this, this weird life that is mine, are coterminous, then so be it, I don't think I'd change it after all, whatever comes next. It would be a betrayal, as if I were the person who had plunged a knife into his heart when he was only seconds away from home and left him there, on the pavement, his life seeping out of him and nobody around to hold his hand, to tell him it would all be OK, to hang on in there. He was dead by the time someone did come along and I never got to say goodbye.

**

I'd only spoken to him a couple of times, once in school, in the staffroom, and once at somebody's leaving party, but there was something about Richie, even though I hardly knew him, that made it impossible to lie to him. So, when he caught me as I was putting on my coat and asked what I was doing on Friday, I didn't say I was meeting a girlfriend or that I had a prior engagement. Both of these were at least partially true and I may, in other circumstances, have employed them as part of my defence mechanism against further relationship disaster, but I didn't.

"I've been asked to sing a couple of tracks with my friend's band. They are playing in The White Horse," I said, looking at his expression for clues. What would he think about that? Would it seem hopelessly lame, singing with a covers band in a pub? But, no, clearly it didn't, as his face lit up.

"Wow! That's amazing! Can I come and see you? I promise to clap very loudly, and I can do a wicked whistle."

So saying, he put two fingers in his mouth and emitted an ear-piercing sound that caused several people to stop and turn to look at us.

"Sorry," he said, seeing my face. "I won't do it again if you say I can come."

So of course I said yes, it would be fine, but it didn't feel like a proper date as he winked and said he'd see me there and that was that. So, even though he didn't turn up, and for a while I thought it would never happen, that's where it became a possibility. From that moment, I couldn't be in a room with Richie without registering it. Even when I was angry with him and trying to ignore him, he was on my radar.

I have to be honest, though. Most of the butterflies were due to the fact that I was about to sing with Olga's band in what was now a scarily short time. What on earth was I doing? How had it got to this point of apparently no return? I loved Olga, she was a really good friend and we had known each other since we both started the same postgraduate teaching course, but she did have this capacity to sweep people along with her own bright enthusiasm for life and suddenly you would find yourself involved in an activity way out of your comfort zone. If it hadn't been for Olga, I never would have seen Tibet and Nepal, never would have trekked through the most breathtaking landscapes, never would have slept on a beach in Bali and certainly never would have found myself working in the craziest kitchens and bars so we could raise enough money to make our way back to catch the flight home. I probably would have spent the summer writing lesson plans.

This little escapade had started when we missed the last train back from Birmingham one Friday after a night out, and we figured that it would probably be cheaper to find a budget room than pay for a taxi. That may or may not have been true, as we'd both had quite a lot to drink and our logic was almost certainly impaired, but we managed to find a place only a short walk from the station and resigned ourselves to managing without even a toothbrush. The room was very basic – not like this one is, but in a student accommodation kind of way – but there were two beds and an en suite and it was fine. We'd both drunk enough to sleep well wherever we were.

The next morning, I grabbed the shower first. I didn't feel too bad, considering, and I was happy. I remember that, being happy in a carefree way, although it is a long time now since I have felt anything remotely like it. It wasn't anything in particular, it was just life being positive. I was young, I was healthy, I had just started a job that I loved, even though it was hard going at times, and I was here, with my friend, having a laugh. My biggest problems then were having no deodorant and no clean pants. That's probably why I was singing in the shower. It was something I did from time to time and I didn't think anything of it, but Olga did.

"Amy Barker, you have a seriously good singing voice," she said as I emerged from the bathroom, wrapped in the obligatory white hotel towel. I don't remember what I said, something deprecatory no doubt, as I never was much good at taking compliments, but she continued.

"No, seriously, I'm not bullshitting. You can really sing. Have you ever, you know, done anything with it? Been in a choir? School concerts …?"

Clearly I hadn't. I knew I could sing in tune, as I could feel my voice matching the notes of the music from a very early age, but nobody had ever suggested it was anything more than that. I felt myself blushing, which was ridiculous at my age, and told Olga not to be silly and to get on with her shower or we wouldn't be out of the room by 10.30am.

But, although she complied then, she mentioned it again later and it became something of a theme over the next couple of weeks so eventually I began to believe it might be true. Was it possible that I actually had a talent? I had always been such an all-rounder, good or good enough at almost everything, that I had never really expected to be especially good at anything, but maybe I was. Maybe this was something I could shine at. I found myself singing more and more when I was alone, and I memorised the words of some of my favourite songs.

So that's how it started, and one thing led to another, what with Olga's tenacity and irresistible energy and my embryonic self-belief, and it was only a matter of weeks before I was persuaded to come along to a band practice. This was on a Sunday, and I would normally have spent the afternoon preparing for the week ahead, so I had to get up early and get my planning completed in the morning. I was nowhere near being confident enough to walk into a lesson without knowing exactly what I was going to do - to the extent of rehearsing the words I would use with some classes - and I would never have risked falling prey to the incipient unrest of the Year 9 middle set, however exciting the notion of band practice seemed.

When I arrived at the venue – it was the back room of The White Horse, soon to be the scene of my debut although I wasn't even considering that possibility at the time – the others were all there and I was introduced. I recognised a couple of them from nights out with Olga's crowd, but I doubt we had even spoken until that point. There were five of them, including Olga: Tim, lead guitarist and singer; Becky, who played keyboards and a number of other odd instruments; Ali, the drummer; and Anton, whose prize possession was an enormous double bass, taller than he was.

They were a friendly bunch and greeted me with smiles and nods, but I could see they were keen to get on so I found a chair near the back and settled down to listen. The called themselves The Butterfly Effect, and I had seen them play before - of course, how could I not, with Olga the lead singer. - but I was interested to see how they arrived at the fairly polished performance I had witnessed.

It was clear almost from the start that Olga and Anton were the driving force behind the band. It was they who had come with new songs to try out and it was Anton, in particular, who reined them in when the laughing and joking went on for too long. In half an hour they had perfected the couple of songs they started to learn the week before, and made a start on two more, and I was very impressed. So impressed that I had completely forgotten the reason Olga had invited me, and was simply enjoying the music and watching the dynamics within the band when they stopped playing and Olga beckoned.

"Come on then, it's your turn," she said, jumping off the little stage. "You haven't come just to sit there doing nothing!"

My heart gave a huge bump and started to race. This was obviously a very bad idea after all. I had never sung in front of any kind of audience, let alone an audience of musicians who couldn't help but be critical. However, Olga was not about to listen to any of my protestations, and dragged me up to the front and stood me in front of a mic. There then followed protracted negotiations about the song I would sing, as every one of her suggestions sounded ridiculous. How could I even think about trying to emulate Aretha Franklin or Tina Turner? In the end, we decided upon the old Gershwin song 'Summertime' as I didn't associate it with a particular female singer who could reproach me for murdering her song. I took a deep breath.

I didn't know all the words, and Olga joined in with me at first, a bit like a karaoke DJ will do sometimes with a nervous singer who has been bullied into taking part. But then I got into it, felt my voice growing strong, felt the music in my ears and the vibrations in my throat. It wasn't until later that I realised that Olga had stopped singing and left me to it after only the first verse. It was like the day I learned to swim, when Dad told me he had actually let go of the back of my costume halfway across the pool and I had swum the other half unaided. I could sing, and the smiles and ripple of applause from the other band members told me this wasn't simply Olga being kind.

Still, that was all I could manage on that occasion. I was shaking, with relief partly, but something else too, a kind of electric feeling as if something was about to happen to me. I told Olga about it later, as we walked out to the car park.

"Ah, it's the buzz," she said, nodding sagely. "Better than drugs and even harder to kick. Now you've felt it, you'll want to feel it again. How about next week? Same time, same place?"

She was absolutely right. I couldn't stop thinking about those few moments when my body and the music had entered into some kind of fusion; when the mic had seemed like an extension of my own arm. There was no question that I would go again, and I spent every spare minute of the days that followed trying to memorise the songs in their list so I wouldn't have to reject so many next time round.

And so this became almost normal. For several weeks, I would work hard on Sunday mornings, go and join the band in the afternoon and sing a song or two. Sometimes Olga and I would sing together, her much deeper voice complementing mine, but I would always sing at least one song alone. Just me and the rest of the band, with Olga standing in the middle of the room with a smile big enough for a whole audience, her approval practically tangible. I loved it, and my nerves were gradually replaced with a feeling of huge satisfaction and pleasure. I was very grateful for this experience, and I hoped they wouldn't get tired of me taking up their time, but I had no thought of it going any further. That's why what happened next was such a surprise, so completely out of the blue.

"We've got a gig here in a couple of weeks," said Olga, as I helped her carry equipment out to the van.

"That's good. You should get a decent crowd here."

"Yes, it's always a good night. That's why we thought it would be a good choice for your debut," she said, heaving an amp into the back of the van with a grunt. She said it as if she were talking about covering a lesson or being on gate duty. Something you just did. Nothing to get excited about. For a moment I wondered if she'd actually said it at all, but she must have, for now she straightened up and carried on the conversation as if I'd already replied.

"Just a couple of numbers, we thought. Something you know really well, so you won't have to think about remembering the words. What do you think?"

What did I think? Well, I thought she had probably gone mad, or maybe that she was teasing. I thought that I could never, ever, make the huge leap from singing with friends to singing to a whole room full of strangers, however nice a crowd they were, but then I had a fleeting image of the band, all lit up on the little stage, and there were people crowded at the front, some of them dancing, and I was there too, next to Olga and sharing her mic, belting it out. Aretha Franklin, 'Say a Little Prayer'. We'd tried it out just now, just half an hour ago. Could I really do it?

Somehow, it was agreed. I didn't even argue much, although I regretted it when I got home, but by then it was already a fact. The next Sunday, they worked their way through their list in a businesslike way and left a good chunk of time for my two songs, one with Olga and one on my own. They sounded good, I knew they did. There was never any discussion about whether it would actually happen, it was only a question of when, and they decided I would sing the last number of the first set with Olga, then kick off the second set with my solo song.

"Before you have a chance to change your mind," said Anton with a smile.

I could have changed my mind. I had nearly another full week to think about it, and I did seriously consider it, more than once, but somehow the days passed without any decision being made and the closer the day of the gig came, the more unreasonable it seemed to pull out. Mostly I didn't have time to worry about it anyway, as the Headteacher was convinced that the school would be inspected at any time, certainly before Christmas, and suddenly a culture of fear and panic seemed to descend on many of the staff. Even more work, even more scrutiny. Sometimes a whole day would pass without a single thought of the gig, and then it would hit me, as the last child left the last class of the day. Oh my God. Haven't I got enough bloody stress in my life? Why am I doing this to myself?

But then there were also the happy reveries as I drove home and imagined my song going down well, heard the applause and even the odd whoop of appreciation. I was never going to miss this opportunity, not really, and if I'm right and everything else flowed from that gig, well actually it all started weeks before that, in the shower of a cheap hotel room. That was my very own butterfly effect. The beating of tiny wings that would stir up a storm. And what a storm it would turn out to be.

So that's how I got to be rushing around like a crazy person on a damp Friday afternoon, dumping my school work in a corner, showering, dressing, looking at my reflection in horror, undressing, dressing again, applying make-up, swearing, wiping it off, applying it again. I was like a silly teenager on her first date, my heart pounding away and my stomach churning. Behind the fear and anxiety there was a little thrill of anticipation at the thought of Richie being in the audience, but mostly that was completely swamped and, when it did pop up, I told myself it was only casual, it had never been a real date. He probably wouldn't even come.

The early part of the evening passed in a blur. I was aware of a trickle of people coming into the room as the band finished setting up and carried out a sound check. I was aware of the lights that flooded the stage and of all the kit sitting there, like some kind of deformed, electronic copse: the spindly saplings of the mic stands, the guitars leaning against their stands like stunted little trees doomed to failure and the cables snaking around everywhere like creepers. Olga and the others were at the bar, enjoying a quick drink before it was time to start but I could not stomach the thought of anything, let alone the fairly substantial glass of wine that Olga set on the table in front of me.

"OK chick?"

I nodded, and thanked her for the drink, but it must have been obvious how nervous I was, so she sat down beside me and gave me a little pep talk. Everyone, she said, feels the same before their first performance, but once you are up there, it all falls into place. She told me to enjoy it, which did not seem likely, and told me how good I was.

"We wouldn't have invited you to sing with us if we weren't sure you could do it, isn't that right Tim?" she called. Tim joined us and said the same thing, and then Anton and the others, and I was bombarded with encouragement until Anton looked at his watch and announced it was time to start.

To be fair, they were only a pub band. They played covers and they mostly did it for fun, to give themselves a creative outlet away from their jobs, all of which were stressful in their own ways. They didn't compose their own songs and there was no musical genius amongst them, but they were pretty good at what they did. They knew their audience liked to hear familiar songs, but didn't mind if they were given a new treatment, so they pushed this as far as they could with some songs and left others more or less alone, to produce an eclectic mix that was pretty well guaranteed to leave the average pub audience happy. That was the aim and it had seemed fairly simple a few weeks ago, as I sat at the back of the room and watched them rehearse. Now it seemed a lot less certain.

One by one, the band played the songs on their list. The audience were appreciative insofar as there was a ripple of applause at the end of each number, but nobody was dancing yet and most people were sitting in groups and chatting, only pausing to clap politely when convention demanded. This was quite normal for a first set, and the playlist was designed to recognise it. Most of the faster and more popular tracks were saved for later, when the audience would have had a few more drinks and might be in the mood for dancing.

I was quite grateful for this as, inexorably, my slot drew closer and closer. Maybe they wouldn't even notice my presence. Three more songs and then it's me. Two more songs. This song, and then I have to stand up, walk across the space that has been cleared for dancing, climb onto the stage. What if I trip? What if I freeze? I had barely even thought about Richie, so caught up was I in the moment, in the excitement and the anxiety of it all. And anyway, people often came later to these things didn't they, I told myself on the couple of occasions the thought rose to the surface.

And then, suddenly, it was time. Olga introduced me but there was no obvious response from the crowd. I managed to walk across the tiny dance floor without incident even though it appeared to have expanded to the size of a cricket pitch, and then I was behind the mic with Olga and we were singing. Just like that. I can't describe it properly, even though I thought about little else the next day, but it was as if someone had thrown a switch in my head. Click. One minute I was a nervous wreck, convinced that I would chicken out when the moment came for me to sing, and the next I was belting it out with Olga, our cheeks almost touching. I may not have been Aretha Franklin, but I was giving it my best shot.

Just like in the lyrics of the song, that moment will stay in my heart forever, even though without it I probably wouldn't be lying on this bed right now, trying to quell the waves of panic that could so easily overwhelm me. Trying to think it all through, just in case my memories provoke some tiny little clue about what went wrong and what I can possibly do now, now that I am on my own with no Nat to protect me. No Nat to shore up my defences, to make it all OK.

Despite all this, I still treasure that moment when the song ended and there was more than just a ripple of applause. I hadn't been able to see it whilst we were singing, as the lights were in my eyes, but now, as Anton announced the break and the stage lights were replaced by the wall lights around the room, I could see that people were looking at us, exchanging a few words, nodding their heads. They had liked it, and Olga gave me a huge hug as I stood there, bright spots from the lights still dancing in front of my eyes and my blood coursing through my veins at twice its normal speed.

"That was fantastic!" she said. "Can't wait to see what they think of the next one!"

That was the thing about Olga. She was absolutely lacking in any kind of mean-spirited jealousy or self-interest. She had a great voice and I wasn't any threat to her position, but it wouldn't have been surprising if she'd felt a little put out. The only song that had aroused any interest in the audience was the one that I had been involved in, but she was delighted for me. I still get a lump in my throat when I think about the fact that I have lost her now, and that she never understood why it had to happen. I wonder if she still thinks of me, or whether she has erased me completely, a person not to remember, a person who rejected her friendship and support and pushed her away.

I was really buzzing then and, although of course I was scared, I was also excited about my song. It was a Bob

Dylan track, 'Knockin' on Heaven's Door', but with a soft, slow, dreamy arrangement that really suited my voice, so Anton said. Its other advantage was the fact that it was very easy to remember, with only two verses and a highly repetitive chorus, so there was little chance that I would forget the words. Nothing could go wrong, and, when at last it happened, nothing did. I sailed through it, and I could tell that the room had grown quieter, that some of the people standing at the bar had turned sideways to watch. I could see Olga out of the corner of my eye, standing to the side, and I could see her hands held flat together, her fingertips touching her mouth in silent supplication. I saw her almost jump, and clench her fists in pleasure as I finished, and I heard the applause, louder than before. I even heard a couple of little whoops and whistles, just as I had imagined, and it took me a moment to remember that I had to stop then, to step away from the mic, leave the stage and go back to being a mere part of the audience. A few hours ago I had imagined my relief when it would all be over, but now I wanted nothing more than to stay where I was.

I spent the rest of the second set basking in a warm glow only partly tempered by the fact that Richie obviously wasn't going to turn up. Nothing, not even being stood up by someone who was pretty nice to look at and had seemed like a genuine guy, could spoil my enjoyment right then. It was a good night, as predicted, and there was quite a crowd bopping away at the front as 11 o'clock approached. The pub had a strict rule about finishing by then, as there were historical difficulties with neighbours' complaints about noise, but there was such a clamour for an encore at the end of the last number that the landlord held up a finger to indicate one more and the audience cheered and clapped. I clapped too, but then I noticed a few people turning to look at me, still sitting at my table to one side where I had been joined by Anton's girlfriend and Tim's wife.

"They want you," someone said, and then, before I knew it, I was back on stage next to Olga and we were singing. I didn't know all the words, but I knew the chorus. It was 'Girls Just Want to Have Fun', that old Cyndi Lauper classic, and I think the rest of the room knew it too.

And didn't I have fun! It was a couple of minutes before the audience gave up and realised that the landlord's impassive stance, arms folded, indicated a man not to be moved. Nevertheless, there was a lovely feel-good atmosphere in the room as we left the stage to get a quick drink before clearing up, and several people stopped us to say how much they had enjoyed it. We found a table recently vacated by a large group, and pushed all the empty glasses to one side, but I had barely sat down before I realised that I hadn't been to the toilet the whole evening. Now that I had relaxed a little, my body was demanding to be heard.

"Sorry," I said, squeezing past Anton. "Won't be a minute."

The ladies toilet was right at the other end of the pub, down a long corridor behind the bar area, but I knew where to find it because of all the Sunday afternoon practice sessions. I wasn't really looking where I was going or thinking about anything other than what had just happened. If I closed my eyes, even for a few seconds, I was back on stage again, feeling the thump of the bass and the heat of the lights and the tickle of Olga's hair on my shoulders as we leaned in together to sing. I washed my hands and looked at my reflection in the mirror. I looked exactly the same, if a little flushed, but I knew it was a different me standing there; a subtle change had happened up there on the stage and I gave myself a little smile to show that I knew it.

I was probably still smiling as I dried my hands and opened the door into the corridor, and just as the door swung shut behind me, someone came out of the men's toilet and stood there. He was smiling too.

"You were amazing tonight," he said. "I've seen The Butterflies loads of times, but you really added something. Have you sung with them before?"

He was a nice-looking guy, about my age or a bit older. Dark blonde hair in an artfully tousled style, faded T-shirt with some kind of logo on the front, jeans. He wouldn't have stood out in a crowd and he probably didn't look unlike a number of other young men in the audience that night, but he had lovely, white, even teeth and it would have been difficult to get past him in that narrow space without completely ignoring him or being rude. Besides, Richie hadn't turned up, I was in a good mood, and here was someone who wanted to say nice things about my singing.

I smiled back.

"Oh, thanks, I'm glad you enjoyed it, but actually it was my first time."

"Oh. Well it worked, really it did. I'm not just saying that. Who were you with before?"

I told him it was my first time, not just with The Butterfly Effect but at all, my first time ever, and his eyes got rounder by the minute. I noticed they were a beautiful colour, an unusual grey with flecks of blue and green. I said 'yes' when he asked if he could buy me a drink, and I hurried back to the others. Would it be OK if I had a quick drink with someone? I'd only be ten minutes or so and I'd help with the clearing up afterwards.

"That's fine, take all the limelight and bugger off, we don't care!" said Anton with a smile, and there was a bit of good-natured teasing from the others, but Olga took my hand and squeezed it.

"Go for it, girl," she said, "and take as long as you like."

Olga knew I'd had a succession of doomed relationships in the past two years since splitting up with Arif, my long-term boyfriend from sixth form. The cultural difficulties between our families had defeated us in the end, and I'd had my heart broken. Everything that had happened since seemed designed to prove that he had been the only one I would ever really love, despite Olga's predictions that ideal men were like buses, you only had to wait and any number would come trundling along.

I smiled and squeezed her hand back, and there he was, at the bar. I felt a funny little lurch of something – disappointment, I suppose – that it wasn't Richie standing there waiting to tell me how much he'd enjoyed the night, but I pushed it to one side. It was his loss, and if he couldn't even be bothered to turn up I was probably well shot of him.

He bought drinks, and we looked around for somewhere to sit. The pub was emptying fast, even though they were still serving, so I pointed out a table near the stage, as far away as possible from Olga and her encouraging smiles, and we sat down.

"I know I said it before, but I have to say it again. You've got a quite remarkable voice," he said.

"Thanks."

"No, really, it gave me the shivers – in a good way, of course. Are you going to be a regular now?"

I told him I didn't know. Although it was pleasant to receive such glowing plaudits it felt a little over the top, and I really had no idea whether the band would want to include me again. I tried to change the topic of conversation, asked him the usual kind of things, but I didn't get a great deal in response, only that his name was Greg and he worked in IT. By that time, I could see the band beginning to unplug the equipment and wind up the cables, so I swallowed the rest of my drink and thanked him.

"I'd better go. I can't leave them to do all the packing up, but it's been nice talking to you."

"Oh, do you have to?"

I was standing by then, and I nodded. Yes, I really did have to go, but he looked so sad that I found myself agreeing to meet him again. Just for a drink, just so we could finish off the conversation, he said. I could see Olga glancing across at me, and because I felt guilty about not helping and guilty about taking a drink from him then leaving so quickly, I arranged to meet him the following Wednesday after work, at a pub in town.

There was an awkward little moment when I thought he was going to try to hug me, but it turned into a handshake and then he was gone. His hand had been warm and a little damp, so I ran my palm over my thigh.

"He seemed nice," said Olga.

"Yeah, I guess."

"He's a good-looking guy. No spark there?"

"Maybe," I said. There hadn't been a spark, not really, but I'd agreed to meet him now. I would see what happened on Wednesday and take it from there. Everyone told me I gave up too easily on relationships, dismissed people before I'd had a chance to really know them, so this would be a chance to prove them wrong.

The weekend passed in a blur. I cleaned the flat, washed clothes, planned lessons; I did all the normal things that had to be concertinaed into a weekend and had a night out on Saturday, but all these familiar tasks were completed in a new, unfamiliar context that was me as a singer. It sounds completely ridiculous as I think about it now, but I felt like a different person. I had to keep looking at myself in mirrors as I sorted clothes or tidied up the week's debris. Who was this person looking back at me?

And the flat, my precious flat. That thought has made me remember it so clearly. It was hardly a flat at all really, just two rooms and a bathroom, but it was the first place I'd lived in completely alone and I loved it. It was my little haven, away from the chaos of student life and the unending misery of my parents' house. The day I left it, the day I picked up the last box and loaded it into the back of Richie's car, I almost cried, even though I was deliriously happy to be moving in with him.

But that is jumping on too far, too fast. The weekend passed, and then it was back to school. There, I would still be the same Miss Barker as I'd been when I drove out of the gates on Friday. No amount of praise for my singing would provoke the Year 7 class into showing a glimmer of interest in Romeo and Juliet unless I taught it well and instilled something of my love of the language into my teaching. I had to put these silly, vain thoughts to one side and concentrate on my job. I was not going to be a famous singer – most probably not any kind of singer at all – but I did want to be a good teacher. This is what I told myself as I drove to work that morning, along with some other stuff about trying to avoid Richie McCowan. It wasn't that I cared, it was simply that it might be embarrassing.

I sorted out the materials for my first lesson, checked the smartboard was working, checked it again, then headed off to the staffroom for a quick coffee. Clearly my body was paying absolutely no attention to what I had told it in the car, as my pulse was racing even before the shot of caffeine, and I knew what that was all about. Would Richie be there and what would happen if he was? I refused to exclude myself from the staffroom on his account, but really. Why did I feel so anxious?

A surreptitious glance around the staffroom told me I was safe, so I made myself a coffee and sat down at the end of one of the rows of metal-framed upholstered seats. There was the usual hum of conversation, people coming and going with piles of books and laptops under their arms; the usual moans and groans of a Monday morning. Nobody bothered me, and I drank my coffee and pretended to look at my phone whilst the clock inched towards 8.30am and registration. I was just about to get up and rinse my cup when I looked up and saw Richie. He had seen me and was walking directly towards me. There was no escape.

"Amy, I'm so sorry about Friday! Did it go well?"

I shrugged and leaned forward to gather my things from the low, wooden table in front of me. This meant I could avoid looking at him without blanking him altogether.

"Yeah, it was fine thanks."

"Look, I'm really sorry. I wanted to let you know, but I don't have your number, or any way of contacting you. My dad was taken into hospital and I had to take my mum up there – she was in such a state she couldn't drive – and it was all a bit hectic. I'm really sorry."

What could I say? There was no reason to disbelieve him, so I said not to worry and I hoped his father was OK, but it was all very cool and stilted. The staffroom was emptying as everyone went off to registration, so we parted then, with formal thin-lipped smiles that were imbued with finality. Whatever there had been, it was gone now, if it had ever existed and even if it wasn't his fault, I was meeting someone else on Wednesday so it was too late anyway. That's what I thought as I hurried off to my tutor group, although if the way my heart was pounding was any indication, I didn't seem to be entirely convinced.

***

I have to stop this now or the tears will exhaust me. Those precious days. Sometimes there is comfort in them, but not now. I have to do something, as the light is fading outside and then he will come, I know that. He is so clever, he will have gone to work as usual, acted normally, done his job with no hint of what is in his mind, but he will be secretly relishing the thought that now he has me. And then I will hear the lock turn and he will be there. Will he smile as if I have come willingly to this place, as if this is some hotel room assignation he has dreamed of? Or will he be angry that I have resisted him for so long, thwarted all his attempts to win me with love, made him resort to force?

I can't bear it, I have to make some sort of stand, so I get to my feet and work my way round the room again. There must be something I can drag across to the door. A barricade, that's it. It won't be a long-term solution, as I can't get out if he can't get in, but it will keep me safe until the police find me. It won't be long before Nat comes to the flat, and he'll be anxious enough, knowing what I was going to do today, so maybe he will be earlier than usual. But even if it's early evening, when he rings the bell and I don't answer, and then when he lets himself in and I'm not there, then it will all start. The police will be round at Greg's house in a flash, and, even if he's out, if he's here, trying to get in, it won't matter. They'll be going through his stuff, confiscating his computer, grilling his parents. Something will give it away.

So, what I'm doing is buying time. I have to remain calm, I have to be practical. I have to believe that they will find me before too long and all I have to do is stay safe in the meantime, so I put my back against each piece of furniture to see if it will shift. I don't really have much hope for the wardrobe, it's huge and does not budge an inch, but the fridge-freezer seems like a good proposition until I see that it is fixed to the floor with two strong metal clamps, one on each side. The bedside table can be moved, but it is flimsy and light, so that only leaves the single dining room chair, the desk and the bed. I take the chair across to the door, but it is too short to fit under the handle in the way that I have seen people do in films, so I take it back and sit down. Would the bed be heavy enough to withstand someone pushing hard from the other side of the door? It's only a single bed, and it looks new. If only it were a great, big antique thing like the wardrobe, but it's pine, probably a self-assembly kit, with a tiny headboard.

I get up and try to drag it across the floor. Maybe, if I put the desk and chair on top of it, it would buy me half an hour or so. But it's no good, he has obviously thought of that, as now I see that each leg is attached to the floor with a metal bracket – those right-angled steel ones, with a total of six screws to each – so that's another option gone. That just leaves the desk then. What can I do with that? It doesn't appear to be fixed to the floor, so I drag it across to the door and push it up close, as close as I can. Then I bring the chair and put it on top, hoping to wedge it under the handle, but the desk is too tall really, and I can see the slightest movement will dislodge it.

I stand back and try to imagine the door opening. None of this is going to stop anyone for any time, but what if there could be something under the door, something wedge-shaped, that would prevent the door opening suddenly and pushing my barricade to one side? In my mind, I can see what I'm looking for, the kind of wooden or plastic wedge that people use to keep doors open, but there won't be one in here so I will have to improvise.

I'm off on my travels around the room again, like a bloodhound on all fours, seeking out the means of my salvation. Of course there is no ready-made wedge, but what about the plates? They are made of hard plastic, and that doesn't break easily, so I try forcing one under the door but I can't see it working; it is too flat, and it will slide across the carpeted floor if any force is exerted. I turn to the wardrobe. This is one area I have yet to examine in any detail, as the sight of all those nearly-familiar clothes gives me the creeps, but I go through each drawer in turn. Maybe there will be a nice leather belt that I can fold up and push into the space under the door, maybe, maybe …

There is nothing. Just clothes. Nice clothes, new clothes, clothes that I could have chosen myself, and hangers that are fixed to the rail, like they have in hotel rooms, so you can't steal them. It's hopeless, there is nothing here, nothing in the bathroom either, so I am going to have to hope that the police pull him in before he has a chance to get here. I will sit on the bed and wait for him, that's what I'll do, and if he breaks down my barricade I will talk to him, tell him it won't be so bad for him if he does not hurt me. I will tell him that I won't press charges, that it has all been a big mistake; a misunderstanding. I will try to buy time that way, but the thought of him trying to kiss me, to hold me, will not go away, and I sit up against the headboard, my arms around my knees, staring at the door and thinking about how different it could all have been if only I had never agreed to meet him for that drink

***

Looking back, it was clear from the start that it was never going to happen – me and Greg – but I was not in the mood to accept that then. There were so many reasons why I wanted it to work, for him to be the one who would help me to move on. There was all the history of the past few years, Arif, any number of one night stands and a few that had lasted a matter of weeks – Liam, Jon and others I didn't even care to name. There was Richie, with whom I still felt angry for no apparent reason, Olga, who wanted so badly for me to be happy and Mum, who had taken to asking me oblique and loaded questions about my social life whenever we spoke. It would be such a nuisance if Greg turned out to be just another name in my ever-lengthening list of failed relationships. I had to give it a chance. I had to give it enough air to breathe.

He was already there when I arrived at The Saracen's Head in town. It was 5.30pm and there were a few people in the lounge bar but not many. Not enough that I had to spend any time scanning the room anyway, for there he was, at a table for two in one of the little alcoves. He jumped up with a huge smile when he saw me, then bounded across the room and led me across to the table, as if he were the lord mayor of some little place in the middle of nowhere and I was a visiting dignitary from a much bigger and more prestigious twinned town.

He hurried away to get me a drink, and I noticed with a slightly uneasy feeling that there was a single rose, wrapped in cellophane, on the bench seat where he had been sitting, but I pretended not to have seen it when he returned and handed it to me. I could have sworn he even made a little bow.

"Something beautiful and precious for someone beautiful and precious," he said, and I almost laughed until I saw that he was deadly serious.

"How lovely," I said, berating myself for my mean-spirited thoughts. Any other girl would think it was sweet; a kind and thoughtful gesture. Why did I have to think it was creepy? It was no wonder none of my relationships worked when I was so jaded and cynical.

But, to be fair to him, that was the low point of the evening and Greg did not continue to make me feel uncomfortable. We chatted quite easily about music and books, finding that our tastes overlapped in many ways, and I told him about teaching. He was a good listener. He laughed when I described the many mistakes I had made on various placements the year before, sympathised when I told him about the never-ending lesson observations that blighted my life and asked sensible and thoughtful questions about working with challenging children. Before I knew it, a couple of hours had passed, but when he picked up our glasses to return to the bar for the third time I decided enough was enough, even though I had only been drinking soft drinks.

"Greg, it's been a lovely evening, but I have lessons to prepare before tomorrow and I really should get back," I said.

I bent down to pick up my handbag and, as I straightened up again, our eyes met and there was that sadness again. This guy really likes me, I thought, and that was something that hadn't happened for such a long time that it gave me a twinge of pleasure – that and the soulful grey eyes with the blue and green flecks. They really were beautiful eyes. That's probably why I agreed to see him again at the weekend, and as I had already arranged to see a film with Olga on Saturday, we decided he would pick me up from The White Horse after band practice on Sunday and we'd have a roast.

"Leave it to me, I'll sort it out," he said, so that was that. It seemed harmless enough, and I was actually thinking of all the positives and half-persuading myself that there was something there after all as I drove home. If only I'd known.

By the time Sunday came, I was less enthusiastic. I couldn't put my finger on it, but there was something about Greg, something indefinable, that didn't work for me. He was good-looking, clean, totally polite, interested in everything I had to say and a non-smoker. He liked many of the same things I liked, but I had no feelings of pleasurable anticipation in the days leading up to our next date, and that wasn't good. I'd have been counting the days, even the hours, if he was going to mean anything to me, I knew that. But I had no method of contacting him and I wasn't going to miss band practice, so I told myself it wouldn't do any harm to see him. I would have dinner with him, insist on paying for myself, then make it clear it wasn't going any further. I had never given him any reason to think otherwise, and although it would be awkward, it could hardly break his heart. After all, we hadn't even kissed.

Although I'd seen Olga a couple of times, it was the first time I'd seen the band since the gig, and they were all there, already set up and jamming when I arrived, fifteen minutes late. It had taken me ages to choose what to wear, something that would be suitable for what I assumed would be a decent pub or even a restaurant, but wouldn't look as if I was dressing to please him or appear remotely sexy. In the end I'd chosen a really dull dress, black tights and flat shoes and I could feel the surprise in the room as I took off my coat. I looked as if I was going to visit a very strict and old-fashioned aunt.

"I know, don't say anything," I said. "It's a long story. Another episode in the very dull and sad history of my love life, I'm afraid."

Olga laughed and jumped off the stage to hug me.

"So you were right after all. He's a non-starter?"

"I think so. I'm going to have this meal then tell him – unless I feel differently by the end of it."

"Well, there's no telling what a nice piece of rare beef can do," said Olga, which made me laugh, and then she pulled me up on stage. "Come on, that's enough talking. We've got a new song for you."

The rest of the afternoon passed in a flash. Obviously I wasn't up there on the stage all the time, as they had to practise their standard numbers and a couple of new ones in preparation for Christmas, but it was clear that my inclusion wasn't short-term. They talked about future gigs and how my songs could fit in as if it had already been decided. I was part of the band – a small part, admittedly – but, it seemed, I could fill a gap that they hadn't really known existed. That was assuming I was happy to continue?

Of course I was more than happy, and I told them that. I suspect my face had given it away before I had a chance to say anything, and I smiled so much that afternoon that my cheeks were hurting by the time we finished. I had barely given Greg a minute's thought the whole time, but as we packed away the equipment and I looked at my watch, I realised that I really didn't want to see him at all. I wanted to finish off here, go for a drink with Olga and the others and return to my flat, even if that meant some kind of makeshift meal rather than a nice Sunday roast. I was trying to think of an excuse that would not sound completely lame and unconvincing when a head popped round the open door that led out to the car park.

"Hello, can I steal your singer?"

I hadn't had the opportunity to say anything to Olga, let alone the others, so they all said yes of course they would finish off the packing up without me, yes of course I should go now, they would manage perfectly well without me. So all my excuses disappeared before my eyes, burst like iridescent bubbles in the air, and I found myself following him out to the street.

"My car's just down here," he said.

I told him I had driven here, said that I would follow him, but he insisted on driving me, saying he wanted me to relax and that he would drop me back here afterwards. It was silly, but I just didn't have it in me to argue the point, knowing what I was going to do later. If it came to it, if he took it badly, I could get a taxi from wherever we were going back to The White Horse and I would never need to speak to him again. I hoped it wouldn't come to that, as he was a perfectly nice guy, but this was definitely the last time, however amiable he was and however attractive his eyes were. That is what I was telling myself as we drove through town and out into Merrifield, about three miles away.

"Are we going to The George?" I asked when it became clear where we were heading, but he smiled and shook his head.

"No, not The George."

I couldn't think of any other food pubs in the area, certainly not any that would still be serving by this time on a Sunday, and a little worried feeling appeared in my stomach.

"It's just ... Look, I'm sorry Greg, I should have said before, but I can't be out too late tonight as I've still got a heap of work to do. I meant to do it this morning but I slept in. Are we going far?"

Still the enigmatic smile.

"No, don't worry, we're nearly there," he said, taking a sharp left down a small side road. Was there a pub down here? Maybe he knew of some little hidden gem, a locals' pub that served a good, hearty and traditional roast, so I relaxed a little as he manoeuvred his way between the many parked cars and finally pulled into a space near the end. I couldn't see anything even vaguely resembling a pub, but I assumed it must be reached via some little alley or lane and I picked up my bag in anticipation.

"OK, here we are. I hope you don't mind, but we're going to eat with my parents. Everywhere was booked up, and I wanted you to meet them anyway."

I have no idea whether my face reflected the true extent of my horror at this prospect, but if it did, Greg chose to ignore it and got out of the car. I was still sitting there, trying but failing to think of anything that would get me out of this, when he came round to my side and opened the door.

"Come on then, let's get inside. It will all be ready by now, and Mum hates it when I'm late."

It was a drizzly November late afternoon and already dark, but I could see we were heading towards one of a small number of identical houses. They were local authority stock, constructed from some kind of concrete blocks rather than bricks, and I recognised them as similar to those in a street in my parents' village. Of course this was nothing that would have concerned me in itself, but the house we were approaching was festooned with Christmas decorations even though it was still another week until the start of December. A sad-looking Santa leaned drunkenly towards his friend, a fully inflated snowman with a sinister smile. He was guarding the other side of the front door, and between them, they almost blocked the entrance to the small porch. Various bells and stars winked and flickered in every window and another version of Santa in his sleigh, complete with numerous reindeer, was picked out in lights across the front of the house.

"We love Christmas here," said Greg, somewhat unnecessarily, but I swallowed the sarcastic response that had popped into my head and said something about liking it too. I didn't say this with any emphasis or enthusiasm. It was a polite, throwaway comment, but Greg seized upon it as if it were the most significant thing I had ever said.

"Oh, that's great! I'm so pleased. I've been worrying about it, you know, that you'd be one of those bah, humbug types who sneer at people who like Christmas. My parents would celebrate it all year round if they could afford it, so they'll be delighted you love it too."

What could I say? I did like Christmas. Admittedly only in the way that most people like it, but there was no point in contradicting what I had said a few moments before, and I could think of no words to express what I thought about displays like this – certainly none that wouldn't have been downright insulting. So I said nothing as Greg tried to get Santa to lean in the other direction and rummaged around for his keys.

We entered a tiny hallway, hung with yards and yards of tinsel that swayed gently with the breeze from the open front door and snaked up the narrow stairs in front of us, twisting and curling round the banisters in a riot of different colours. Greg took my coat and hung it with his, on some pegs at the bottom of the stairs.

"We're here!" he called, and a door opened to reveal a small, round, white-haired woman with rosy cheeks. She was wearing an apron with a Christmas pudding emblazoned on the front and a flashing reindeer badge. Her earrings were tiny little Santa hats.

"Oh, Billy, we were wondering where you were," she said with what I guessed was mock sternness, then she waited whilst Greg introduced me and we shook hands. Billy? Why the hell had she called him Billy? I was beginning to feel seriously uncomfortable by now, and I even considered making a bolt for it, there and then, but how hysterical that would have seemed; how embarrassing.

"Come and meet my father," said Greg, guiding me towards the room from which his mother had appeared. "I'm afraid he can't walk very far these days."

We went into the room, which was a lounge-diner, crammed with a shiny new-looking leather three piece suite at one end and a round dining table at the other. It was stiflingly hot, with a gas fire on full and the smell of cooking making it seem quite airless. Greg's father was a frail-looking man, almost bald and very thin. His hands were twisted with arthritis, but he had a lovely smile and I could see the likeness to Greg.

"Pleased to meet you, my dear," he said, giving my hand a squeeze. "The boy has told us a lot about you. Seems you're quite a little songbird!"

I blushed, muttered some kind of self-effacing nonsense and sat down on the sofa beside Greg. There was a lot of clattering coming from the kitchen which led off the lounge by a door at the back, and when Greg's mother called for his father to come and help, he rose from his chair with difficulty and hobbled off, leaving us alone. Now was my chance.

"Why did your mother call you Billy?" I whispered.

"Oh, it's just a family name," he said. "My middle name is William, but my mum actually wanted that to be my first name, so she started calling me Billy when I was little and it stuck. I'm Greg to everyone else."

Relief flooded through me. What he said had a clear ring of authenticity about it, and I could just imagine his funny little mother taking matters into her own hands and calling her baby by the name she preferred. It actually suited him better, and just for a fleeting moment, I had a vision of me calling him Billy at some point in the future. But that was a future that would never happen, of that I was sure, and even the thought of it made me feel queasy. These were nice people, there really was nothing to worry about, but they were never going to become part of my life.

In a matter of minutes we were summoned to the table. I had half-expected a turkey with all the trimmings, given the devotion to Christmas, but it was beef. I had to suppress a smile when I remembered Olga's comment, as this particular joint was well done to the point of being a little tough, but the rest of the meal was actually rather good. The potatoes were crispy, the Yorkshire puddings were fluffy and the vegetables were just how I liked them, with a little bit of bite. We ate with very little conversation and I was the first to clear my plate. I put down my cutlery and sat back with a satisfied sigh.

"That was absolutely lovely. The best roast dinner I've had in ages," I said, with only a small and excusable degree of exaggeration. Greg was beaming from his place opposite me and his mother reached across and touched my arm.

"You're very welcome, my dear, but this is nothing. Just wait until you see this table at Christmas!"

Fortunately, my response to this was so immediate that there was no opportunity for it to be filtered by any notions of politeness or convention, or I have no idea how the conversation would have progressed. It was bad enough as it was.

"But I won't be here for that!" I said, and then I saw the expression on Greg's face. If looks could kill, his mother would not have lived to see another Christmas, let alone cook the dinner, and she turned a deep red.

"Oh, I see. It's just that Billy, I mean Greg, said ..."

"No I didn't," said Greg, "I said 'if', Mother, not 'when'. I said 'if Amy comes for Christmas dinner'. I never said she was coming for sure. I haven't even asked her yet!"

There was a terrible moment of silence, broken only by the sound of Greg's father resolutely sawing his way through a particularly tricky piece of beef with hands that were too bent and deformed to hold the cutlery properly. I had to do something, so I told them that my own parents would be expecting me for Christmas and would be hugely disappointed if I did not come. This was only partly true, as I was hoping to spend as little time as possible there on Christmas Day, but it seemed like the best thing to say at the time.

"Of course they'd be disappointed! I can't imagine what we would feel if Billy suddenly told us he was having his Christmas dinner somewhere else. We'd be devastated, wouldn't we George?" said Greg's mother, and then she turned to her son.

"Billy, I'd like you go and check on the pudding for me. And when you've done that, I suggest you go upstairs and put your glasses on. Your eyelids are swelling up."

Suddenly, Greg seemed to have shrunk. He slumped in his chair like a moody adolescent, and then he sighed, stood up and left the room, shoulders down.

about all that, my dear," said Greg's mother s. "He gets a bit carried away sometimes. He's not a bad lad though, and we couldn't re devoted son. He bought all the furniture in this room you know, and he always pays his keep, regular as clockwork. We thought we'd never have any children, but then along he came, out of the blue, and he has never given us a moment of trouble since the day he arrived!"

I had no idea how to respond to this. Greg's mother appeared to be telling me that her son, who apparently still lived at home, was a bit odd but basically harmless and good-natured. This did not seem like a very strong endorsement of him as boyfriend material, but I was not concerned about that at the time. I was concerned about how much longer this ordeal would last and how I could get Greg – who wasn't my boyfriend and was never going to be – to drive me back to The White Horse without first consuming pudding.

"Ah, there you are, that's better," said Greg's mother as he returned. "I don't know why you wear those stupid contact lenses when you know they make your eyes sore. Anyway, go and get the dishes from the sideboard, there's a good boy, and I'll bring it in."

Greg did as he was told like the good boy his mother said he was, then sat back down opposite me. I glanced up and only just managed not to gasp out loud when I saw that his eyes, behind his glasses, were an innocuous light brown. Gone were the stunning grey irises with the green and blue flecks, sitting, no doubt, in a little pot on a shelf in the bathroom. It didn't matter, not by then, but I couldn't help feeling slightly cheated. Would I have chatted to him, had a drink with him, on the night of the gig if he'd been wearing his specs? Obviously I was a very shallow person, as the answer to that was quite probably 'no.'

I had to eat pudding. It was a bizarre experience, as we all sat there and ate generous portions of lemon sponge and custard as if nothing untoward had happened. Greg's father asked me about my school, how many different classes did I have to teach and were many of the children naughty? His mother asked about my parents, as if she was still weighing me up as a potential daughter-in-law, and Greg joined in by answering some of the questions for me. I was mildly surprised at how much information about my life he had retained, a fact that should have rung some alarm bells but didn't, especially as there were some things I could not remember having even discussed.

Fortunately, the focus on my job enabled me to exaggerate my very pressing need to get home and write lesson plans, and Greg, having made quite a long speech about my dedication, could hardly argue with that. Of course I offered to help with the washing up, but there was unanimous agreement that I was a guest, and therefore exempt from that particular task. In any case, his generosity seemed to have extended to the installation of a dishwasher, so I could leave with a clear conscience. There was only the car journey to endure, and the necessity of making absolutely sure that he had got the message. This was not a relationship and that was that.

I said goodbye to Greg's parents with relief but no animosity. Hands were shaken, cheeks were kissed and thanks were exchanged. They probably knew it was the last time they would see me, but we kept our farewells bland and general and then I squeezed between the two inflatable icons outside and followed Greg to the car. As we set off, I decided to take the initiative and lead the conversation for as long as possible, so I extolled the virtues of his mother's cooking and complimented the warmth and cosiness of their home. I even provided him with a little more information about my own life, by comparing his parents' obvious affection for each other to my own parents' interminable cold war. I talked almost without pausing for breath, not daring to stop for fear of what he might say if I did. I talked as if my life depended on it.

At last, the illuminated sign of The White Horse appeared at the end of the street and I felt myself relax. Only a few more minutes and it would all be over. My bag was on my knees, so I made a point of searching for my car keys and holding them in full sight.

"Door to door delivery," I said with false brightness as he indicated left and pulled up, directly behind my car. "Please say thanks again to your parents, it was a great meal, and it's been ..."

"Yes, it's been great, hasn't it?" said Greg, completely failing to realise where I was heading, or if he did, failing to admit it. "How about a drink one night next week?"

My heart sank. This was going to be more awkward than I had allowed myself to hope.

"I'm sorry, Greg," I said, forcing myself to meet his unremarkable eyes, "but I'm not looking for a relationship at the moment. My life is so taken up with teaching that I barely have time for my friends and the band, and it wouldn't be fair to you. I'm going to say goodbye now. It's been very nice to meet you, but I have to say 'no' to the drink. Sorry."

I opened the door and started to climb out of the car, but I didn't get away that easily. "We can be friends though, surely," he said.

How was I supposed to respond to that? I could hardly say no, I don't want to be your friend, you are beginning to give me the creeps and I hope I never see you again. So I said something that was anything but enthusiastic without being entirely negative. Something like 'of course' or 'why not?' I was so keen to get away that all my focus was on that moment when I would be able to swing my legs around and plant my feet on the pavement. Shut the car door. Watch the tail lights disappearing into the night. I really can't remember my exact words, although I've tried often enough, desperate to work out whether I inadvertently encouraged him, but really, in all but my craziest moments, I know it always comes down to the same thing. I could have told him to fuck off and die and he would still have come back for more.

Not that I knew that then. I honestly thought it was all over as I closed my front door and leant against it, almost laughing out loud with the joy of being back in my own space. Human beings don't like being rejected, and although I thought he might feel sad, or angry, or even that I had led him on, I really didn't think I would see him again. It was like people who meet on holiday and exchange email addresses. We must keep in touch, oh, yes, we must, and if ever you are in Leeds, or Leicester or Norwich or wherever they are heading back to … Everybody says it, but nobody really expects it to happen. Certainly not when the plane has landed and the harsh reality of a suitcase full of dirty clothes and work in the morning hits them. That's what it will be like, I told myself. He will drive home, and maybe he'll think about me for a day or two, but he won't really believe we are about to start up some kind of shared social life. He's not stupid, whatever else he is.

Luckily, the story about lesson plans was exactly that: a story. I had completed all my preparation that morning, including the discovery of a neat little presentation downloaded from a resources site. That had saved me an hour or more, so I had plenty of time to text Olga.

I'm back. Seriously weird evening!

Olga wasn't keen on long text conversations, she much preferred the spoken word, so my phone was ringing within seconds. I'm not especially proud of the way I portrayed Greg's parents and their house, how I turned them into caricatures, how I reduced her to tears of laughter when I described the poor semi-inflated Santa or how that led to silly innuendo about Greg's possible sexual prowess or lack of it. It was unkind and snobbish and they didn't deserve it, even if Greg himself was fair game, but I suppose it was my way of dealing with it. Joking about it made it seem less serious and helped to disperse the horrible creepy feeling I had still not managed to throw off completely.

"Well," said Olga, "I suppose that's the price of fame and you'll have to learn to live with it, but I've still got a pile of marking to do, even if you are Little Miss Organised. I'll see you on Sunday if not before, and thanks for the laugh!"

Nothing else happened for two or three days. I went to school, taught my lessons, came home. More often than not I fell asleep in front of the television as soon as I'd eaten, before waking up and forcing myself to work for another hour or two and collapsing into bed. I had seen Richie looking at me across the staffroom once or twice, but then I also saw him sharing a joke with one of the PE teachers – him leaning in and her tossing back her raven hair – so I guessed he was keeping his options open. In any case, I was too tired to worry about him, and the experience with Greg had put me off relationships altogether, at least for the time being.

It was later in the week that I sat down with my laptop just before bed. I tended to use my phone to keep on top of things, but this was the first occasion I'd had time for a proper browse. I deleted my emails – almost all of them were junk – then turned to Facebook. There were two new friend requests, so I accepted them both, almost without thinking. It seems like madness now, knowing what I know, but in those days it all seemed so benign. I had hundreds of friends, many of them people I had never met, but they were friends of friends and what possible harm could it do?

Then I saw what I had done and my stomach lurched. Gregory Payne. If he'd called himself Greg I may have paused long enough to think about it, but now it was done. I really didn't want him seeing my posts, checking out my photos or worse still, messaging me, but what could I do now? I could hardly unfriend him again that quickly, it would look strange, so maybe it would be better to go along with it for a while. He'd probably lose interest before long – after all, he was a good-looking guy, smart, well-dressed. He may not have been my type, but surely some other girl would like what she saw and enjoy his company?

I went to bed, but now the uncomfortable feeling was there again, lurking in the background. I told myself not to be so stupid, after all, he'd waited all this time before making contact. If he had been thinking about nothing else I would have received the request long before this, but the feeling didn't recede. It was like waking from a dream in which something has gone horribly wrong but you can't remember what it was – a tight, anxious feeling, dissociated from reality but difficult to shift. I didn't know it then, but if this was a dream it would turn out to be a nightmare from which it would be very hard to awake.

December 23rd

He didn't come. I don't know how, but I fell asleep eventually, and – although my dreams were all about that door, and how I managed to open it, or how somebody came and let me out with a garbled explanation that made perfect sense at the time – I seem to have slept for hours. There is a morbid, grey light seeping through the window and I think it must be dawn, so that would make it about 7.30 or 8am I suppose. This time yesterday, I was waking up with an excited feeling in my stomach, like a little girl going to a party. My first trip into town for months, and I was going to buy Nat something nice for being so fantastic. Now he will be half out of his mind with worry, and I doubt he will have slept even as well as I did. He probably spent half the night at the police station hassling them to get a move on and find me, but they haven't, not yet.

So what do I make of this? Does it mean that Greg has been arrested but won't say where I am? That is scary, as if he never tells anyone, I suppose I will die of starvation, eventually. There is enough food to last for a couple of months, especially if I ration it, and running water, so it would take a long time to die, but it is possible. A slow and horrible death.

Then there is the possibility that he did not return home after bringing me here. I still don't remember a thing about it as I must have been heavily sedated after the initial attack, but he could be somewhere in this building, biding his time, or somewhere else where nobody knows him and the police will never find him. Then, providing he is careful, he will be able to come to me whenever he wants, and I will be at his mercy. Would that be a fate worse than death? I don't know.

And I must consider the possibility that it was never Greg at all, not since Richie died, anyway. Could it really be that the police were right and Nat was wrong all that time? Could it be some random stranger? If that is the case, I have no idea what I could be facing, and that prospect is worse than the other two. I have to stop thinking about that, so I think about the good things that may be about to happen. Any minute now, I may hear the sound of footsteps on the stairs, or a door somewhere below being forced open with a crash, and then they will be here. Greg will have told the police where to find me, or they will have found out somehow, and I will be free. Nat will be here too, and I will throw myself into his arms and he will look after me.

How strange it is, to sit here and compare these possibilities. If my life was a book, and somebody was reading about me, they would say, oh, that wouldn't happen! She wouldn't be sitting calmly on the bed working out the relative merits of dying of starvation or being attacked by different men. She would be screaming and crying at the door, throwing things at the windows, anything to get out. But they would not know how strangely normal it feels to be here. I have been a prisoner in my own home for so long, have spent so many hours in minute examination of any number of awful futures, that this is not as strange as it should be. I hate myself for my passivity, but a lot of my fire has been stolen, slowly, imperceptibly over the past two years, and now, when I really need it, it is hard to summon it up.

One thing is certain, I won't be in any fit state to fight or even to resist if I don't eat, so I force myself to choose a breakfast. There is a box of granola – a brand I have enjoyed at home – and even frozen mushrooms, but there is a toaster on top of the freezer so I defrost a couple of slices of bread and nibble away at toast and marmalade. There is no pleasure in this, and I am feeling full and queasy before I have finished, so I push it away and lie back on the bed, waiting for the nausea to pass. For a second, I look around for my laptop, as if I were at home and lying on my own bed. This is what I would do, sometimes for hours, when I lacked energy or when the weight of it all stopped me doing anything else. My laptop was my solace, although, as it turns out, it may have been my downfall too, although I could not have guessed that then.

***

I may have been careful about what I posted for a day or two, but, pretty soon, I almost forgot about Greg's friend request. There was absolutely no evidence that he was even looking at Facebook, and he certainly never posted anything or made any attempt to contact me. So, I had been worrying about nothing after all, and Christmas was only a few weeks away, with its round of parties, meals and other social occasions, so I was upbeat and happy. I had one more gig with the band to look forward to, and the only cloud on the horizon was Christmas Day itself, when I would have to sit in the crossfire whilst my parents sniped at each other from their respective armchairs. I was trying not to think about that, as there seemed to be no escape, but at least I could enjoy the rest of the season.

The final gig of the year was back at The White Horse on the second Saturday in December. The landlord had phoned Anton a couple of days after my debut and asked if the band could fill a cancellation, so that was an unexpected bonus and it was likely to be an even better crowd than before, with Christmas so close and everyone getting into party mode. I was a little nervous about singing to what could be quite a large number of people, but Olga told me not to worry.

"To be honest, most of them won't even be listening. They'll be drinking and chatting, laughing and messing about until about halfway through the second set, when everyone will get up and dance. We'll have some fun, but there won't be any music critics there. Just enjoy it. You'll be fine!"

I pretended to agree with her, but I was quite anxious by the time Friday came and the gig was only the next day. Normally, I didn't talk a lot about my personal life in the staffroom, as I didn't want to be like some of my colleagues who walked in every Monday morning and regaled anyone who would listen with the dreary details of their weekends. The barbecues they had hosted, the dinners they had cooked, the many and various antics of their children, all of whom were either highly talented in some field or other or driving them mad. There was no way I was going to be like that, but when Alisha, who was a Maths teacher and also in her first year, sat down beside me and unwrapped her sandwiches, it seemed quite normal to talk about our weekends and of course it all came out.

"Wow, I had no idea you were a singer! You've been keeping that quiet," she said. Obviously, I played it down, said it would only be two or three numbers and that Olga was the real star, but she was clearly impressed and kept coming back to it, even though I tried to steer the conversation towards her. I guessed that must have been when Richie found out about it, as I hadn't mentioned it to anyone else and I don't think we had any mutual friends at that time. I wasn't aware of him being close by, but it was the best explanation for how he came to be at the gig the next day, as all the posters I'd seen still showed the band who had cancelled.

I didn't see him at first. I was getting quite good at setting up the equipment by then, and I was genuinely busy, rather than hanging around trying to be useful as I had been in the early days. I had put my coat over a chair at the same table as before, but I didn't leave the stage until the band were ready to start, as we'd taken our drinks back there to hold a last-minute discussion about the playlist. The pub was getting busy even at this early stage, and Anton thought we should replace a couple of the slower songs with others that were more conducive to dancing. I offered to drop one of mine, but nobody agreed to that, and we settled on Anton's suggestions without much more debate.

So, with some trepidation but an overall feeling of excitement, I climbed off the stage and headed to my table. That's when I saw him, standing quite near to the front with a typical Richie smile on his face and a pint in his hand. My heart leapt, but then it crashed again almost as suddenly, as there, a little behind him, was Greg. I had realised, in that split-second, that I actually did care about Richie being there, and Greg being around was going to mess it all up. He would be watching me, I was sure of it, so how could I talk to Richie, smile the sort of smile that I wanted to, with those eyes on me? I sat down and pretended not to have noticed either of them, forcing myself to concentrate on the music, but without much success.

When the time came for my first song, there was a shrill whistle from somewhere in the audience but I couldn't enjoy it. How could I be sure it had come from Richie? It might have been Greg and that unnerved me. It didn't stop me singing, and there was warm applause as I finished, but I felt as if I had performed with my foot slightly on the brake. I could have given it more and it was all his fault, that stupid, stupid man. Why did he have to come and spoil everything?

Then it was the interval, and we headed for the bar but, unfortunately, a lot of other people had the same idea, and it was ages before we were served. There was certainly nowhere to sit. I looked around for Richie, hoping that he would beckon me over, but he was nowhere to be seen, unlike Greg, who waved and smiled far too enthusiastically. I noticed he was not wearing his glasses, and I wondered if he had an array of unusual lenses to choose from. Maybe his eyes would be bright blue tonight, or green, like a cat's. Hopefully, I would never be close enough to find out.

I could see that Olga thought it was strange, but she agreed to come to the toilet with me when the break was nearly over.

"I haven't done this for a while," she said, as we made our way down the corridor. "Do you want a girly talk?"

"No, it's him – Greg. He's here, and I was worried that he would follow me and want to talk to me. I'm probably being silly, as I know he's been to other gigs, but there's just something about him. The way he smiled at me."

"Bloody hell!" said Olga. "A stalker!" But she was only joking, and I made myself join in with the joke. Of course it wouldn't turn out to be anything that serious. It was just awkward.

My next song was first up in the second set, so we both went straight to the stage. There, I've done it, I told myself. He won't be able to catch me alone now. He was still there, of course he was, but somehow I felt more relaxed now that I'd told Olga and we'd laughed about it together. Richie was there too, and he gave me a thumbs–up. Then the stage lights came on, the wall lights were dimmed and, strangely, for this had not happened before, a hush descended on the room. OK, there were still the sounds of people ordering drinks and a bit of conversation at the back of the room, but a lot of the audience were quietly waiting. Waiting for me to sing.

This time it was the old Lynyrd Skynyrd classic, 'Sweet Home Alabama' – again in the chilled out, dreamy style that Anton seemed to like for my songs. It's a pub band classic and I knew that, but I was not expecting what happened when I got to the first chorus. People were singing along with me – not in the shouty, football-song way that they do sometimes, but properly singing – and this made me tingle. It also gave me a huge boost of confidence, and I really threw myself into the rest of the song, allowing myself to include a couple of things I had tried at home but not in practice; a little pause here, a little throaty 'yeah' there. Looking back, it was probably hopelessly cheesy, but the audience loved it and there were more than a few shouts of approval at the end.

"More from Amy later," said Anton, introducing the next song, and then Olga joined me and handed me a tambourine.

"You may as well stay on stage," she said.

Later, as I lay in bed, far too wired to sleep, I kept replaying that moment. It was the acknowledgement that I brought something to the band, that it wasn't about them indulging Olga's friend and her delusions about singing. The rest of the set had got better and better as the evening progressed, with a great crowd at the front, dancing and cheering wildly at the end of each song. Naturally some of that was down to drink and some of it was down to pre-Christmas bonhomie, but the art of a good pub band is to maximise the goodwill in the room, so Anton said, and that's what we did that night.

And that wasn't all. Richie pushed his way right up to the stage when the encore was over and caught my eye. He crooked a finger and mouthed 'please?' so I sat down on the edge of the stage whilst the others put down their instruments and turned off the amps. After all, a tambourine doesn't need a lot of maintenance.

"You were fantastic," he said.

"Thanks."

"I'm so glad I came. I nearly didn't. I thought you might not want me to, but then I thought, oh, what the hell. I'll hide at the back."

"You didn't hide at the back though," I replied. There was a little smile hovering around my lips and it matched the one on his.

"No, would you have preferred me to?"

"It's a free country," I said, but I was smiling properly now. I couldn't help it.

"Does that mean I can buy you a drink?" he said.

I couldn't see any reason to refuse. The others were trooping off to the bar and there was nothing to do for a while, so he bought drinks and we stood by the stage as there was still nowhere to sit. I won't say that I had completely forgotten about Greg. I did scan the room for him from time to time, but mostly I was still on such a high that nothing could spoil it. It was only a drink and a chat, but I could tell that Richie did like me after all and, there was no denying it, I liked him too.

Nothing more had happened. The time came to clear up, and Richie had said goodbye, see you on Monday, in a fairly casual way, but it was enough. There would be no more avoiding him in the staffroom. No more awkward moments or pinched smiles. What would be would be, but I had that warm feeling inside that told me life was good. Greg had obviously been there to see the band rather than harass me, and the fact that he had smiled so broadly simply meant there were no hard feelings. Result.

By the time Monday came, I was still buzzing. Olga had phoned to say how well I'd done, so that was good, but in my hierarchy of things to feel happy about, Richie was number one. We can't help the old biological drives, can we? In terms of achievements, the audience response to my song should have been way up there at the top, but the fact that Richie had come, had talked to me, had looked at me in that certain way, had kept it down at number two. The apparent resolution of the Greg problem was there at number three, slightly ahead of the rapidly approaching school holiday and the chance to relax and catch up on lost sleep. With so many things to feel happy about, even the thought of Christmas Day with my parents did not seem so bad.

The remaining days of the term flew past. There were some difficult moments, times when I struggled to control classes that were becoming increasingly demob happy, but mostly, I coped. It was comforting to know that I was not the only one, and I was able to join in with weary conversations around the coffee machine in the knowledge that this was part of the deal. Teaching is often an uneasy truce between joy and anxiety, but as long as the joy outweighs the anxiety, you carry on. I only wish that was all I had to worry about now, whether the noise from the

Year 9 class would filter out into the corridor, or whether enough of them would pass the end of term test.

The staff Christmas party was directly after school on the last day of term. The pupils would be let out early, and then we would have an hour or so to remove all evidence of Christmas from our tutor rooms before sharing a buffet and some drinks. It was more or less obligatory to attend, as the Head liked to show his appreciation for our efforts by buying a few bottles of wine and making a very dull speech. That is what Richie told me the day before, on one of the several occasions since the gig that he had sat beside me in the staffroom for a few minutes. The conversations had been friendly but nothing more, and I wondered sometimes if I had misread the signs at the gig, but at least we were talking.

That's why I spent some time deciding what to wear on the morning of the last day, and put my make-up into my handbag. I even thought about taking my straighteners, but decided that would be too much. Apparently it was common for people to leave their cars at home if possible, and the younger ones would often head into town and get wasted in a succession of pubs and bars. Would Richie be part of that crowd? Would he ask me to come with him?

As it happened, events overtook us and that was all decided well before the end of the day. When I arrived at school, the receptionist stopped me and handed me a huge bouquet of flowers.

"Here, these came for you, about fifteen minutes ago. It's lucky I was here," she said, as if it was my fault they had been delivered at such an inconvenient time.

I thanked her, picked them up and took them to my tutor room. How lovely! I was hoping they would be from Richie, although it did not seem very likely, or maybe it was something to do with the gig. Maybe they were from Olga and the others. There was a little envelope tucked between the blooms, with my name on the front and a card inside.

'Something beautiful and precious for someone beautiful and precious,' it read, and my blood ran cold.

Suddenly, whatever emotion I had been feeling at that moment – fear, suspicion, anxiety – was replaced by another: anger. How dare he do this? How dare he intrude into my life when everything was going so well? He had no right, no right at all, to expect me to receive these flowers with what? Thanks? Is that what he was expecting? I had given him absolutely no reason to expect anything from me at all and he could fuck off. That's what he could do.

I almost growled aloud as I crammed the flowers, head first, into the bin and squashed them down, but it was hopeless as it was a fairly small bin and most of the stalks, together with a lot of the cellophane wrapping, protruded from the top. The more I pushed them down, the more they sprang up again, until I sat down on the floor with my head in my hands. I couldn't leave it like this, the kids would be bound to see it and then there would be a barrage of questions.

"Miss, why are them flowers in the bin?"

"Miss, did you fall out with your boyfriend? Did he cheat on you?"

"Ahh, look at her. Bless! She's all upset!"

I didn't hear Richie come in. If I had, I would have leapt to my feet and tried to push the bin out of sight, but as it was, he was witness to my despair and there was nothing I could do to hide it.

"Shall I go away again?"

I looked up, and part of me wanted to make a pretence that everything was fine, but it was overwhelmed by the apparently greater need to burst into tears and tell him the whole thing. There was a moment when I thought I'd blown it, as he, naturally enough, thought there was some kind of relationship between me and Greg and didn't want to get mixed up in anything complicated. But when I told him what had happened, he was sympathetic and sat me down at one of the tables.

"Look, do you want someone to cover?" he said. "We've only got ten minutes until the bell, but I could say you suddenly felt sick, or dizzy or something."

I didn't want that. It was the last day of term and I had cards for my tutor group, each with a little chocolate snowman or Santa inside. I wanted to hand them out myself and, besides, it was only a bunch of flowers. I was over-reacting. I shook my head and said I just needed a couple of minutes to fix my face and look respectable, then I would be fine.

"Thanks for listening, though. I bet you think I'm completely flaky now, don't you?"

"No, I don't think that," he said, and then he patted me on the shoulder and gave it a brief squeeze. "I'd better go, and so had you, but I'll catch you later."

So that was when it all started properly, and who knows what might have happened if Greg hadn't sent those flowers? I might not have been in my tutor room when Richie came to find me, I might have been in the staffroom, having a coffee. And our paths may not have crossed during the day, and maybe the PE teacher with the raven hair – such a dark, glossy black that sometimes it almost appeared blue – maybe she would have made a play for him after a few glasses of wine and then who knows? I like to think that he already felt enough for me to reject her advances, but if she'd been draped around him just as I stumbled across them in a corridor – well, the chances are I would have gone home in a huff and then … Well, there is no point in pursuing this, but maybe I have to thank Greg for Richie; that's all I'm saying.

The rest of it seemed to happen as if it had all been decided at that moment. I saw Richie only briefly during the day, but when we assembled in the staffroom for the Head's Christmas motivational address, he came and sat beside me and we were simply together from that point. I don't even remember discussing it. It was as if we both knew and understood what was happening without the need to express it in words, and I had an amazing feeling of calm, and relief, whenever I looked up and saw him by my side. Naturally, I also had the butterflies and increased heart-rate that are the staples of the start of a new relationship, but it was different this time. It was like coming home.

We left the party as soon as we could without causing too much comment but, again without any real discussion, we headed to Richie's car which was parked in a side street so he could collect it the next day if he'd had too much to drink.

"Do you want to go into town?" he asked, but I shook my head.

"Not really. Somewhere quiet, where we can talk."

"It's quiet at mine," he said, with a little smile, and we both knew that was the perfect idea.

The rest is history. It all is, of course, but that evening is engraved in my mind like fine carvings in a cathedral, even if those memories will die when I do. We didn't fall upon each other as soon as we closed the door, but we started the journey that would only end when he fell prey to the random madness of the street. Poor Richie. Poor me. We couldn't know what was in store for us. We felt as if we had our whole lives before us, and even if we weren't expressing it then, I think we both believed that we would be spending them together.

I didn't say a word about any of this to my parents, when I finally forced myself to appear at their house on Christmas Day. I didn't tell them that I had seen him a couple of times since, or that we had spoken every day. I didn't tell them that I was floating on a cloud of happiness, even though I was still being careful about what I said on Facebook and Twitter, the spectre of Greg still lurking there in the background. If they were different people, they would have seen something in me when I let myself in, laden with bags, to face the inevitable reproach.

"We thought you might have been a bit earlier than this. Your mother has been cooking for hours."

"Happy Christmas, Dad," I said brightly. "Yes, I'm sorry, I meant to, but I was out late last night. Sorry, Mum."

Mum presented me with her usual excuse for a smile and told me not to worry, so I ignored the tone of her reply and busied myself putting presents under the plastic tree, chatting about the weather, which was unremarkable, and school. This was, at least, one subject they would struggle to imbue with negativity, as they had both been teachers themselves and had wanted nothing more for their only child than that she would follow in their footsteps. Growing up, it had been such a part of my life, as it stretched out before me, that it had become a reality almost without my knowing it. It was something of a minor miracle that I loved it, that they had been right.

So, it was no surprise that they didn't notice how happy I was, any more than they would have noticed if I'd been sad. Emotions were not discussed in our house unless it was absolutely necessary, so nobody remarked upon the sparkle in my eyes or the glow on my cheeks and I wasn't going to spoil it by presenting them with the opportunity to find a fatal flaw in my rosy vision of the future. I could imagine Mum's lips pinching together in the way that always heralded a criticism. Deep lines had formed around her mouth, although she had never smoked, carved out by a lifetime of disapproval.

"Are you sure that's wise?" she would have said. "It will be very difficult if you split up, being in the same school."

Or something like that, I don't know. I didn't give her the chance to think of some other reason why Richie and I would not be happy together, because I knew we would be. I knew it with a certainty I have felt about little else, and that got me through the rest of the day unscathed.

As I remember, it wasn't as bad as I had feared. There appeared to be a lull in hostilities between my parents, most of the time anyway, and they seemed to like the presents I had bought them. Naturally, their gift to me was destined to sit in my bedroom until a decent enough period had elapsed for me to take it down to the Oxfam shop, but I had expected nothing more. Dad left all the Christmas shopping to Mum, and she relied entirely upon a catalogue that featured a range of young women wearing middle-aged women's clothes, so there was little hope of a happy outcome there. I smiled as I held up the horrendous lilac jumper she had chosen for me, and said all the right things. If we all lived long enough, maybe the Christmas would come when I would wear such a thing, so at least there was that to look forward to.

Richie laughed when I showed it to him the next day. We hadn't been able to see each other for several days, but now, as we sat snuggled up on the sofa in my flat, we shared our respective family Christmases and vowed this would be the last time we would ever spend Christmas Day apart. That's how it was. We'd only been together a matter of days, but we were able to talk about being together in a year without any feelings of awkwardness as if one of us was rushing things or making assumptions. I got a little shiver when I remembered how I had felt when Greg's mother had talked about Christmas dinner. That had only been a couple of weeks into the future but it had felt creepy and intrusive. Now here we were, still getting to know each other, but in no doubt about how that would happen. I pushed Greg and his mother out of my mind and leaned closer into Richie.

"I think I quite like you," I said.

The rest of the holiday passed as holidays do. Quickly. New Year was a mad round of his friends and mine, as we were both at that stage when you are desperate to show off your new love to everyone you know, and there was nothing to burst our bubble. Olga was delighted, and told Richie he'd better be nice to me or he would have her to deal with, laughing and hugging us both as she did, and then we left that party and went on to another at about 11. He whisked me around, smiling this huge smile and introducing me to his friends, some of whom I recognised but none of whose names I could have remembered then. That was almost certainly the first time I met Nat. I'd had quite a lot to drink by that time, and although I love him to bits, Nat isn't the kind of bloke I would normally even register, but I'm sure he must have been there. He was Richie's best friend and they had known each other since uni, so I can't see them being apart at New Year.

So, that was the holiday over. I had been single at the start of it, and now I wasn't. I had been a mess, worrying about something that, almost certainly, was much less significant than it seemed, and now I hardly thought about it at all. I arrived at school early, full of optimism and enthusiasm, and picked up the contents of my pigeon hole on my way up to my tutor room. I could see that there were a number of envelopes, almost certainly containing cards from pupils, and I wondered how I should acknowledge them, now that I had taken all the others down from the pin board. Should I display them on my desk just for a day or so?

I was still mulling this over as I opened them and glanced inside. I decided to say a personal thanks to any that were from children in my tutor group but to take the others home. It was very unlikely that pupils from my English classes would even remember they had sent me a card, let alone feel let down if I failed to mention it.

It was the third or fourth card that I opened. Even before I had looked inside, it had struck me as being rather elaborate for a pupil to have sent, but I had only vaguely registered this when I read the inscription:

To Amy,
Wishing you a very happy Christmas. I hope you liked the flowers. I am looking forward to seeing you sing again in the New Year, and I know our paths will cross.
Much love,
Greg

My first instinct was to tear the wretched thing into pieces, hurl them to the floor and stamp on them, but I didn't. Maybe because I was feeling so positive, I was able to stop myself and read it through again. What did it actually say? There was nothing really threatening about any of it, when I analysed it phrase by phrase. He wished me a happy Christmas – fine. He wanted to see me sing again – fine. He had sent me some flowers – not fine, but hardly anything I could complain about. The only part that resisted all my attempts at a positive spin was about knowing our paths would cross, but even that could be ambiguous. I replaced the card in its envelope and put it in my bag. Maybe I would show it to Richie later.

I tried, I really did, but I could not forget it as the morning progressed. It was like knowing I was carrying around an unexploded bomb, and I found my stomach lurching every time my eye settled on my bag. Eventually, I put it in a cupboard, but that only transferred the anxiety from one inanimate object to another, and then I found myself trying to ensure that the offending piece of furniture was always behind me, teaching from a strange position to one side of the room. It wasn't a great lesson and I knew I couldn't go on like that, so when break came, I grabbed my bag and went to find Richie.

"This was obviously sent some time ago," he said. "Look at the language. 'Wishing you a very happy Christmas.' That's a wish for the future, or it would say 'I hope you had a happy Christmas,' so it's at least a couple of weeks. Agreed?"

I nodded.

"We weren't together then, were we? As far as he knew, you were still a single girl. He liked you – I get that – and he wasn't going to give up that easily, but if he finds out you're not single any more, my guess is that he'll back off. It's what I would do."

"You wouldn't fight for me?" I said, affecting a pout.

"No, not if I found out you were with somebody else before we had even kissed. I'd go away and lick my wounds, but I'm not a caveman and I doubt he is either, from what you've said. He's just a bit sad. Let's find a way to give him the information and see what happens. I don't think you will hear from him again."

It sounded reasonable and I hadn't got a better idea, so I agreed and, that night, I posted a selection of photos of me and Richie at various events during the holiday. Me and Richie, arms around each other and holding glasses of fizz at New Year; a close up of our two faces, smiling the stupid smiles of people newly in love; me laughing at something off-camera and Richie with his head turned to me, smiling. All those smiles, and more. I almost felt guilty as I chose them, knowing that Greg couldn't fail to feel hurt, but I had to do it.

"You have to be cruel to be kind," Richie had said with uncharacteristic lack of originality, "otherwise he will just go on thinking he has a chance and he will never move on."

Later, I checked Facebook and there were many likes and quite a few comments in response to my post. This was news to some of my more distant friends, and they were happy for me and wanted to know more. I spent some time on one more post then went to bed. There was nothing from Greg and no way of knowing if he had even seen my status, but I had done all I could do and now it was a matter of waiting. I didn't know it then, but I would not have long to wait.

The gates to the car park were always open from about 7.30am. Anyone could drive in, but then they were closed a bit later to prevent parents clogging it up as they colluded with their offspring to avoid even the shortest walk to school. That's how Greg was able to park in a space I could not avoid passing on my way to the entrance. That's how he was able to jump out of his car and stand in my path as I hurried in with my bags of books and laptop swung over my shoulder.

"Hello, Amy."

I was too surprised to answer, but I stopped. Maybe I should have tried to barge past him, told him to fuck off, but I would have needed the advantage of foreknowledge to do that. If I'd had that I would have arranged to walk in with Richie, but I was on my own and off guard.

"I thought you said you weren't looking for a relationship," he said.

I told him I wasn't – hadn't been – but sometimes these things just happen. I don't know what I said, but it all blurted out whilst he stood there, impassive, unthreatening, unwanted, but there all the same. When I finally ran out of things to say he simply nodded and his lips tightened in a thin smile.

"Well, relationships are funny things. Sometimes they last and sometimes they don't, so I just want you to know that I'll be there for you. If, when, you need me, I'll be waiting. I'll see you at the next gig. Goodbye."

"Well, I got that wrong, didn't I?" said Richie, when I told him at break. I had decided not to tell him, to keep it to myself and see what happened, but it was always like that with Richie. It would have been like keeping something from myself, so it all came out, or what I could remember of it, as I found it hard to say what had actually happened. I knew I had said something to Greg, but what I'd said and what I wished I'd said had become somewhat confused. I think I may even have thanked him.

"Still," Richie continued, "it may have been one last attempt. Ill-advised, granted, but understandable, given the rare beauty, intelligence and all-round gorgeousness of the object of his affections!"

"Don't joke about it, please Richie," I replied. I had a horrible feeling of anxiety, like watching the first few minutes of a horror film but without the pleasure. Everything is fine. The sun is shining and there is nothing for the characters to worry about, but you've seen the trailer and you know they will be pulled, inexorably, into something more awful than they could imagine. Now, I know that the logical explanation is that I had probably felt a similar feeling any number of times before, but nothing bad happened and so I only remembered the time when something did. That's what my head believes. But what some other part of me knows is that I had a very strong feeling of presentiment, there in the warmth and safety of the staffroom, with Richie beside me and people coming and going as if everything were normal, so strong that I could not shake it off all day.

***

I remember that feeling. It became quite familiar, and I have it again, or something like it. I know it now as dread, but I did not have a name for it back then. Having felt it for so long, having lived under its cloud, I know that it is a dangerous feeing to indulge. How many days of my life have I lost, waiting for something terrible to happen, and then going to bed knowing that I am another day older and I have done nothing, experienced nothing and yet there was nothing tangible to stop me? This is different, I have no choice but to be here, but I must not sit here all day thinking, I must work on my defence.

Naturally, my barricade is still in place. Nobody has been here to test it, but now, as I look at it again, I realise that it is pretty hopeless. A few hard kicks and the door would push it to one side or topple it over, and I know I must find a way to strengthen it, so I have to think again. I rinse my plate and mug in the tiny bathroom basin and try to make my brain work. I need to look at the situation in a different way, as I have exhausted all the possibilities offered by furniture shifting. There is nothing big enough in this room, but what else might it offer? I will never know unless I try to find out, so I conduct a fingertip search of the floor, starting in the corner by the bed and slowly moving, on hands and knees, along the wall to the corner by the door to the bathroom.

The carpet is fitted but not new, so I prise it up a little where I can and wriggle my fingers underneath. Mostly it is nailed to the wooden floorboards with tacks, so I can't just rip it up, but when I turn the corner to the space where the desk had been standing, I find a tiny coin wedged between the carpet and the skirting board. It is an old halfpenny. I don't remember seeing one before, so maybe it will bring me some luck. There! This room may have other secrets to uncover, and my spirits rise, possibly rather more than would be suggested by such a small find.

The remainder of that wall reveals nothing, and the carpet is firmly tacked down all along that section. However, when I get to the door it seems looser, so I drag my barricade out of the way and pull the carpet from under the metal strip by the door. I can lift it just enough to fit my hand under, and I can feel the dust, dry and gritty, on the floorboards and paper. It is probably newspaper, used instead of underlay, and I pull some of it out, but it is brittle and fragile and I can't see a date or anything useful, so I push it back. I don't want Greg to know what I have been doing.

I flatten the newspaper as best I can, then push my hand a little to each side. There's something else here. It's paper, but it is thicker, smoother, so I tease it out. It's an envelope, yellow with age and grey with dust. It has been opened carefully, with a clean, straight cut along the top, and it is empty. It is addressed to a Mrs E Bellingham at an address in London NW1. The name means nothing to me, but is that where I am? My knowledge of London districts is poor, but I know it must be north of the river, and if that is the case, if that is where I am, what are the chances that anyone will ever find me? I have no connection to London and my flat is at least a hundred miles away. Did Greg ever mention London? I wrack my brains, trying to remember our conversations, but he only ever wanted to talk about me so it is hopeless.

For a while, I sit on the floor with the envelope in my hands. It has taken all my enthusiasm away, but I have to replace my useless barricade, if only to demonstrate that I am not sitting here waiting for him as if it were some romantic tryst. If he is going to have me, at least I will put up a struggle, so even his warped mind will not be able to tell him I wanted it really. I am crying now, as the awful reality of my situation becomes clear. No-one is going to come charging up the stairs to rescue me. I am somewhere in London, the best place in the world to hide, and Greg has had two years to work all this out. He has won, and all our resolve, all Nat's technology, could not save me in the end, as I was the weakness in the plan.

I replace the barricade, then continue my search. I have no expectation of finding anything useful, but at least it passes the time. I cannot move the fridge-freezer or the wardrobe, so those sections have to be missed, but then I get to the bed. I could just about squeeze enough of my upper body underneath to reach the skirting board, but then I have a better idea. If this bed is as new and cheap as it looks, it may not have a solid base, so I drag the mattress and bedding onto the floor and yes, I was right. It's just as I imagined, a rectangular frame with a series of wooden slats at regular intervals from top to bottom. Now I can see the space under the bed perfectly, and I reach through to slide my hand along the skirting board, but all I find is a couple of loose tacks and now I am back where I started.

What do I have to show for my exertions? A coin, two tacks and an empty envelope that may or may not give a clue as to my whereabouts. Mrs E Bellingham may have lived here, but if she did, she may have lived in London previously and brought the letter with her. How can I tell if I am in London? I remove the chair from the barricade and take it to the window so I can peer through the tiny patch of slightly less-frosted glass. Are these the shapes of London houses? Is there anything in the distance, some kind of landmark?

But the answer to all these questions is the same as before. No, there is nothing to help me to know where I am, and what use would it be anyway? Wherever I am, it is Greg who has left me here, and he is most probably planning his next move right now. All along, it has been inexorable, the progress towards this moment, and I should have seen it at the time.

***

There isn't much point in remembering everything that happened in the weeks that followed. It has all become muddled, and it all leads to the same point anyway. What does it matter if the next lot of flowers came first or the hand-made card? What difference does it make when I first saw his car parked in the street at home time? It happened enough after that, but all the time, he was so nice, so pleasant. He never again approached me in person, but he let me know, through all these little acts of supposed kindness, that he was not giving up and that was actually worse in some ways than if he had been threatening.

It was the same with my friends. He had sent friend requests to a lot of them, and several must have accepted him, but what could I do? I didn't want to ask them to block him as it seemed so hysterical, but now he was embedded in my network. Even if I held back on posting, I could hardly expect my friends to do the same, so there were the photos of me with the band, of Richie and me at a party, of the pair of us with a crowd of happy faces as this pub or that club. We had a great social life and the evidence was there for him to see, however painful it must have been. He followed the people I followed and he liked everything that included my name, and there was nothing I could do about it.

It was just after half term that he got hold of my school email address. I suppose he must have called pretending to be a parent and the office staff gave it to him. They wouldn't now – all that was changed – but I didn't blame them. Who could have guessed that anyone would do such a thing? There were occasional messages at first, but they gradually increased over time until, eventually, there were several each week.

Hi Amy,

Just to say I enjoyed the gig on Sat. Great version of Mustang Sally! You and Olga make a great team!
Love as always,
Greg

Hi Amy,

I happened to see you as you came out of school and you looked a bit down. Is everything ok? You know where to find me if you want to talk, or a shoulder to cry on!
Love,
Greg

As if! He was seriously deluded if he thought I would turn to him in times of trouble. I never replied, not once, but still the emails kept coming, and the little gifts delivered to the school, and his car outside the gates from time to time, although it always pulled away as soon as he saw me. I tried to ignore it, but it was beginning to affect me quite badly as the end of term approached. I saw him everywhere, even when he was not there, and dreaded opening up my emails. I actually failed to do so on more than one occasion, luckily with no serious consequences, but I could have got into trouble if I'd missed an important communication. I started arriving at school very early, in case he was in the car park, and leaving later and later, in the hope that he would give up and go home if I delayed it long enough, but nothing worked. Richie became quite worried about me, although I begged and pleaded with him not to do anything. It was all so stupid and embarrassing, and I was certain people would think I was exaggerating. How ludicrous to think I could have a problem with a fan when all I'd done was to sing a few songs with a pub band!

It was a Friday evening, a week before the end of term and we were both exhausted. It was one of the first really mild evenings of spring and we should have been sitting in a pub garden somewhere, unwinding, but neither of us had the heart for it. We sat in my flat, my haven, and tried to decide what to do, but we were stumped. We couldn't go to the police as it all seemed so harmless. What had he actually done apart from praise me, send me presents, offer his support? Surely there could be no law against any of that? We hadn't even seen him at any gigs, although he always professed to have been there, and he hadn't got close enough for either of us to have told him what we thought even if I had agreed to it.

"You know what?" said Richie, sitting forward. "I've had enough of this. We are turning into victims here – well, you are, and that means I am too. We've tried to ignore it, we've made light of it, we've waited for it to go away, and nothing has changed. It's time we took back control."

I asked him what he was going to do and shed tears on his shoulder when he wouldn't tell me, but deep down, it was a relief to feel that something was going to happen. I could start to think about the end of all this, even though I hardly slept that night and was plagued with dreams of being pursued when I did.

The next morning, Richie was on his phone when I surfaced. I could hear him speaking, his voice low and serious, but he wound up the conversation quickly when I shuffled out to the kitchen to see what was happening.

"OK, thanks mate. Yeah, yeah, I know. Will do. See you later, bye."

"Who was that?"

"Nat," he replied, and refused to say more, only that he was going out to see him in a while and that I shouldn't worry.

Of course I did worry. With Richie gone I was jittery and tearful, finding it difficult to do the simplest of tasks and becoming increasingly obsessed by the stalking websites I had started to visit. I had resisted these until now, convinced that they would turn me into a victim when that was the last thing I was going to be, but now I was beginning to realise that Greg's behaviour was typical of many stalkers and that it had to be addressed.

Stalkers. Just reading the word gave me the shivers, and it was so hard to believe this could be happening to me, but the evidence was there and, by the time Richie returned with Nat, I was seriously considering going to the police.

"No need for that," said Richie, when I told them what I had been reading. "Think of all the hassle. You'll have to expose every little detail of your life to them. They'll be in school, wanting to see CCTV footage, emails. They'll grill the office staff about how he got hold of your school email address and it will all be common knowledge in no time. I'm not saying you have anything to hide, of course not, but you're not in a good place right now, are you? And what if the kids get to hear about it?"

He was right, it would be a huge step to formalise all this, and there would be repercussions, but what else could I do? I think I knew what they were going to say, but it made my heart go crazy all the same when they said it.

"We're going to have a word with him," said Nat. "Nothing heavy, I promise, nothing that could possibly be considered threatening. We're just going to tell him to stop, and we're going to do it in front of his parents. Sounds like he's a bit of a mummy's boy from what Richie has told me, and they might support us."

Immediately, I was gripped by the memory of Greg's mother leaning in to me, that terrible evening, with the remains of the Sunday dinner still on the table and Greg upstairs, wrestling with his fake grey irises. How awful for her, for both of them, to be confronted by two strangers accusing their boy of pestering me at best, if not stalking. But then I thought of the alternative, of a couple of police officers coming to take him away for questioning, with the eyes of the neighbours trained on the police car outside the house, watching as they walked down the path and posted Greg into the back seat. That would be so much worse and they didn't deserve it.

"OK," I said, "but you have to promise me, on your lives, or mine, that you will keep it calm. They are really nice people, his parents, and I don't think even he is a bad person. He has a problem, and he's got to stop, but … well, you know. Try to be nice."

They agreed, naturally, and in return I agreed to show them where Greg lived. I didn't know the address, but I was pretty sure I could find it again, and that is what we did, after a late lunch in a pub. We drove there, pulled up about halfway down his road, and I pointed out the house. It looked naked without its decorations and slightly shabby, especially in the light of the spring afternoon. The intention had been to make a note of the number and for Richie and Nat to come back another time, but Greg's car was parked outside the house and there didn't seem any point in putting it off so they got out, slammed their doors purposefully and marched up the road, side by side.

I was sitting in the front passenger seat, so I could see them knock on the door. I couldn't see who opened it, but there was some conversation on the doorstep before they went in, Richie first. Then all I could do was wait and watch, my eyes fixed on the space they had left behind for what seemed like hours, rehearsing what could be happening inside. Would there be a row, would he deny it all or would he break down? What would his parents say? Would they defend him, or would they know in their hearts that this was probably true? These scenarios played on and on, changing and developing until I thought my head would explode and I was ready to go and knock on the door myself, just to make it all end, but then it ended anyway.

In fact, it was only about fifteen minutes before they re-emerged, Nat first this time, to walk back down the path in single file. There were no friendly waves as they went, and the door closed behind them before they reached the end of the path. I could tell little from their demeanour, but Nat smiled and gave me a thumbs-up sign as he approached the car and opened the rear passenger door.

"All done," he said, as if he thought that could possibly be enough for me, and Richie wasn't much more informative.

"Honestly, it's fine. We spoke to all three of them. Explained it was upsetting you, that it had to stop or we'd have to take it further. He blustered a bit at first, tried to play it down, but his mum knew the score, I could tell. It's over, I promise. Now we need to go back and buy this guy a drink," he said, looking over his shoulder at Nat. "I doubt it would have gone that well without him!"

That was all they would tell me and I had to accept it. Obviously I wanted it to be true, but just hearing the words didn't make it so and I still had terrible butterflies in my stomach the rest of that day and, intermittently, for a couple of days afterwards. However, I put on a good show of being relieved and happy and the three of us had a brilliant night out, with as much laughter as I could remember for a long time.

***

The mattress is back on the bed, the bedding has been replaced exactly as it was before and I have hidden my finds at the back of the drawer containing underwear. I can't call it mine, as it isn't, but now I realise I am still wearing the clothes I put on yesterday morning for my trip into town, and I have not washed, or showered, or cleaned my teeth. I have to make a decision. Do I use the things he has provided for me, the clothes, the toiletries? I have eaten his food, but I had no choice in that. Would it be a symbolic acceptance of my status as prisoner, or sex slave, or even partner, if I wash and dress as he obviously wants me to do?

I decide that there is little point in becoming smelly and uncomfortable. With so much else to worry about, the fact that he has bought all these things, carried them here, arranged them so neatly and carefully, is sickening, but boycotting them is not going to make me one bit safer. I decide to wear my own jeans, but I choose clean underwear and a top that is very similar to one that I have at home. It comes from the same shop, and this shows the level of his surveillance. He must have been following me in the days before I stopped going out. He must have been watching me so much more than I could ever have guessed.

I head to the bathroom but now my heart is hammering and I break out in a sweat. Suppose I am in the shower when he comes? There is no lock on the door – obviously – and I will be so vulnerable. He will read something into it, I'm sure – that I am preparing myself for him, making myself beautiful for the moment we have both been waiting for, or some other kind of twisted, deluded nonsense. I imagine him popping his head around the door as he had that time at band practice, then coming in and starting to remove his clothes, smiling, flashing his fake grey eyes, and I retch and lean over the basin. But then I think he will have other, equally twisted explanations for everything else I do, including remaining unwashed, so I pull myself together, turn on the shower and undress, diving in and soaping myself all over in the fastest shower I have ever had. Even when I was running late for school I would allow myself more time than this, but I feel terribly exposed and in danger and I can't see the bathroom door properly through the mist on the screen. I turn off the water and push open the door, my breath coming fast.

I dress quickly. I am not really dry, and I have to wrestle with my jeans to pull them up, but at least I am covered now. I wipe the steam from the little mirror above the basin and look at my frightened eyes, staring back at me. I look ten years older than I did before all this. My cheeks are sunken and there are permanent little creases between my eyebrows. The marks of fear. Nothing very attractive there, I think. Maybe Greg will notice how I have altered and change his mind, but I know that is silly, clutching at straws. If he can imagine that I want him, that the past two years have been some bizarre form of courtship, or foreplay, he will have idealised my physical appearance to the point at which no evidence to the contrary will affect how I look in his eyes. Oh, if only I had looked a mess that night at The White Horse. If only he had taken a shine to Olga. She would have given him the brush-off straight away, and she and I would still be friends.

Without even thinking, I take a cloth from the pipe beside the basin and turn to the shower. This is what I do at home – put the shower gel back on the little shelf and run the cloth around to ensure the walls and the tray are clean. I got into the habit of doing this when I lived in shared houses, and it has stuck. That's when something hits me, and I drop the shower gel with a clatter and sink to the bathroom floor. It is my shower gel! Not the actual bottle, of course, but the brand I always use. Milk and honey for sensitive skin. How did he know that? Suddenly I have a terrible feeling that he has been watching me in the flat as well as outside, as I know I started using this brand after I stopped working. I got a rash all over my back, which was probably nerves when I think about it, but this seemed to help.

I look around and it's all the same. My shampoo, my toothpaste. Even the toothbrush is similar to mine, and panic is really setting in now, as I throw open the door and rush to the fridge and check there, in the freezer, everywhere. There is hardly a thing in this room that does not have some kind of reference to my life in my flat. He has got my whole life on some kind of database, knowing him, and his research is immaculate. It was all so familiar that I didn't even remark on it! What chance do I have against a man who has dedicated so much time and energy to me?

I throw myself on the bed and allow myself to cry, to feel despair. I even drift off into a troubled sleep when the tears dry up, but when I awake the cloud has lifted, to be replaced by a grim determination. I am up against something probably more dangerous than even Nat suspected, but there is still the hope that he is out there, making enough waves for someone to act. I must not give up. Maybe Greg would not want to kill me, having invested so much in making this prison, this love-nest, whatever he thinks it is. Maybe I can keep him calm, even after he has forced his way in.

Now, the light is beginning to fade again. It is that kind of winter's day when there is only real daylight for a short time. Outside, people will be out in the high streets, in the shopping centres, making their way home from work. The warm and inviting lights of the shop windows will be reflecting on the pavements, and may entice some people in, but it is Friday, and many will be hurrying home from work, looking forward to a night out. Maybe they are going to a Christmas meal, or a party. I think about my colleagues at school and wonder how they are. How many will still be there? Many of the younger ones were thinking of giving it up, just like I did in the end, but I wish I was still there now. There is no feeling like the end of term, and I don't know if I will ever feel it again.

***

Things got better and better after the visit to Greg. I was spending so much time at Richie's flat that we decided I should move in and let mine go, and although I was sad, it was another milestone in our relationship, another indication of permanency. I even took him to meet my parents with a remarkable degree of success, and I met some of his family too. By the time we came to the last week of term I was physically tired, but there was still nothing from Greg and I began to believe that Richie and Nat's visit may have worked after all. That meant I was more relaxed, and my last few lessons were the best I'd had for a while, despite the undercurrent of excitement that always precedes a holiday.

Added to that, we were invited to join a group of mostly Richie's friends who had managed to get a last-minute deal on a cottage in Cornwall, so now there was the prospect of nearly a week away from it all. There would be no internet access and the phone signal was intermittent, so it would be only us and our friends.

"You, me, a few mates and a bunch of cows," said Richie, passing over his laptop so I could see the photos on the website.

"It's not a bunch, it's a herd, but it does look lovely," I said, laughing and ducking as he aimed a cushion at my head. I realised then, with something of a shock, that I was happy again. Being anxious and wary had worn me down slowly, gradually, so that I had almost forgotten what I had felt like before, but now it was all over and I could be me again. I could have a laugh, I could be in love and I could enjoy my job. That's what I thought, anyway.

The cottage was amazing. It wasn't what I would call a cottage at all, as it was huge, with enough bedrooms for the three couples and three singles in the group, an enormous kitchen-diner, a lounge, a laundry room and a games room. The central part of the building was obviously older than the rest, and there were extensions to both sides, with the tasteful use of outhouses and barns providing something that seemed just about perfect. It nestled in a natural dip about halfway up a hill, with views across farmland and the sea beyond that. The only disadvantage was the distance from any useful habitation – shops and pubs in particular – but there were several vehicles between us and a shop about a fifteen minute drive away so nothing was too great a problem.

The first day was spent mooching around and doing very little. Some people went to the nearest town to buy food and drinks, and Nat cooked a Mexican meal for everyone in the evening, but I spent a lot of time reading in the garden. Nobody seemed to mind, and I was grateful. The next couple of days were taken up with trips to various beaches and then Nat, Richie and I went to a beautiful little town called Fowey the day after that, whilst others did their own thing. That was the nice thing about that holiday; nobody felt obliged to do anything, and it was a lovely mix of communal living and independence. I hardly knew some of them, but we all got on well, especially in the evenings when we tended to congregate in the lounge or the kitchen with a plentiful supply of wine.

The week went by all too quickly, and we had a barbecue on the penultimate evening. Everyone was there, the weather was dry if a bit chilly and there was plenty to eat and drink. I can remember looking across at Richie as he prodded yet another batch of sausages, and feeling such a rush of love for him that I had to prevent myself from jumping up and rushing across to him, throwing my arms around his neck. His face was slightly illuminated by the glow of the coals, and there were matching rosy streaks in the sky as the sun went down. I took a picture on my phone and it was something I treasured afterwards, after he had gone. Now I don't even have my phone, or my laptop, and I suppose I may never see that photo again, but it will always stay in my memory.

For some reason, I didn't drink a huge amount that night. I don't remember making a conscious decision, but it just didn't happen. Maybe it was because Richie was busy with the food and we didn't spend so much time together or maybe I wasn't in the mood. Whatever the reason, the upshot was that I was one of a very small group of relatively sober people by the end of the evening, and most of the others, including Richie, had staggered off to bed by about 11.30pm, which was very early by our standards. Eventually it was just me, Nat and a couple called Becky and Sam and we spent half an hour or so clearing up the worst of the debris outside and stacking the dishwasher. Then Nat opened a bottle of red and we sat around the kitchen table, the conversation ebbing and flowing. Someone had left an ipod playing on shuffle and sometimes we would stop talking to listen, or to remark on what was playing. I hardly knew Becky and Sam, but they were lovely and I wished I'd spent more time with them earlier in the week, especially as Becky sang in a choir and there was a lot we could have talked about if only we'd had more time.

Anyway, that was how I came to be left alone with Nat. Becky's yawns increased in frequency until she dragged Sam off to bed, but Nat was in the middle of a long story – I can't remember what it was about – and it would have been rude to follow them, so I stayed, but with the intention of saying goodnight as soon as possible.

I don't know how we came to be talking about our childhoods. It was probably me making a joke about Mum and Dad. That was something I did a lot, now I think about it. Better to trivialise their unhappiness than take it seriously, I guess, or to consider the effect it may have had upon me. Anyway, that led to Nat telling me about his own childhood, about the death of his parents and older brother in a plane crash in South Africa, about how he should have been on the same plane but was too ill to travel and how he was brought up by his grandparents.

I think that was when I began to get to know him properly. Of course he was often with us, as he was such a good friend to Richie, but we had never been alone before and certainly never discussed anything personal. Now I found that he was very easy to talk to, a good listener, and that he clearly valued the opportunity to explore some of his own background. Richie may not have been very good at that – he was so resolutely positive about life he would probably have said, "Ah well, that's all in the past now mate! Got to think of the future!" But I love to piece together the jigsaw of people's lives and I am a good listener too.

It's a pity that we opened that second bottle of wine. Although I hadn't been in the mood for drinking earlier, now I found I was enjoying it and I topped up my glass from time to time as Nat talked. He was telling me about being shunted from one family member to another as his grandparents became too frail to care for him. Honestly, it's amazing how well adjusted he is, given what he went through, but it was a sad story and I felt for him.

That was when that song came on and we both looked up at the same time and said the same thing: "Oh, I love this track!" I couldn't help but sing along to it a bit, but Nat didn't. He just closed his eyes. It was 'Street Spirit' by Radiohead, a song that had meant a lot to me in the past and now it transported me back ten years or more whenever I heard it. It was redolent with memories of school and being in love with a boy two years above me who didn't even know I existed. I had played it over and over at the time, lying on my bed and crying adolescent tears, and now it made me want to cry again. In fact I did cry, a little, and it was all rather embarrassing in the end. That's drink for you. It can bring all sorts of things to the surface, as when I looked up, there were tears in Nat's eyes too.

The rest of the Easter holiday passed just as quickly. By the time we had got home and unpacked, done the things we hadn't had time for before we left, marked books, prepared lessons and tracked down resources, the new term was upon us. But I didn't mind, not really. I had thoroughly enjoyed my holiday and I wouldn't have minded it lasting a little longer, but I was also looking forward to teaching without the cloud of anxiety hanging over my head. I knew I hadn't been performing as well as I could, and I knew why, but now all that seemed to have passed. There were no messages on my school email account, no likes on Facebook, nothing to indicate that Greg was continuing his campaign of adoration or whatever it had been. I was free and I was happy.

It was only two days into the new term that we received the notification of an inspection to take place almost immediately. The Head summoned everyone into the staffroom and gave a prolonged lecture about how we should behave and how prepared we should be, but even that did little to spoil my mood. I was a little anxious about being observed, but I was pretty used to members of the senior management team coming into my lessons, and most of my feedback had been positive even when I had been under par. Richie was also quite sanguine about it, but we must have been unusual, as there was a feeling of near-panic in the staffroom. The Head and his minions were running around like headless chickens the whole of that day, with entire classes of Year 7s out picking up litter, new displays in the entrance hall and even advice about dress code in one of the many emails we received.

When it came, the inspection hardly affected me at all. Of course I was aware of the group of suited men and women stalking the corridors but none of them came into any of my lessons and I assumed everything was going well until I went down to the staffroom early in the morning of the second day. I made myself a coffee and slumped down in a corner with the intention of reading through my lesson plan once more, just in case, when I heard voices.

"It's not looking good, is it?"

"Well, what did you expect?"

"I don't know, I thought we might be OK, with the new predictions ..."

"Yeah, well, we all know about them. Inspectors aren't stupid. They can see what's been going on."

It was two of the deputies, and they hadn't noticed me, so I rummaged in my bag, put my headphones in my ears and sat there with my phone in my hand until I was sure they had seen me. Only then did I make a show of packing up as if I had heard nothing of their conversation. Obviously I told Richie later, but we kept it to ourselves and tried to look as shocked and dismayed as everyone else when the Head called everyone together again, after it was all over. He tried to put a positive spin on it, but there was no getting away from it, the interim report showed that the school Required Improvement. It wasn't as bad as it might have been, as teaching had been judged as good, but leadership and management were poor and results in some departments, especially Maths and Languages, were much lower than they should have been.

That judgement may have been the trigger for all that happened later. Maybe if we had scraped through, Richie would not have been in the street that night and everything would have been different. The trouble was, it was difficult to remain positive, even for Richie, whose nature was the antithesis of anything negative, and my renewed enjoyment of my job was short-lived in the culture of blame and increased expectation that ensued. Now we had two headteachers to knock the school into shape: the old one, who stormed around the school with a permanently angry expression, and an 'executive head' who had been drafted in from another more successful school across the city to oversee our improvement. Neither of them seemed to have taken on board the fact that it was not us teachers who had failed and life became an almost unbearable round of departmental briefings, new initiatives and lesson observations, even in my department, which had fared quite well.

By half term, we were demoralised and short-tempered. We spent half our lessons following up petty infringements of the new, rigid uniform code, and the pupils were picking up on the atmosphere of stress with a resultant dip in behaviour. This led to a new and stricter behaviour policy, more exclusions, poor relationships and further stress. Richie and I had more arguments during that time than we'd had in the rest of our relationship. We hardly went out, and when we did, we were often too tired or jaded to enjoy ourselves.

It was a Friday evening when Richie saw it. In the old, pre-inspection days, we would have had Friday evening to ourselves, leaving preparation until Sunday, but now we had taken to working for an hour or two then going out. "Just to break the back of it," Richie had said.

"Look at this," he said, turning his laptop towards me. We were sitting on the sofa, side by side, going through our emails, so I pushed mine to one side and read it. It had been forwarded from the Commonwealth Teacher Exchange Programme, and it advertised the fact that they had a few late vacancies for Science teachers in Canada for the new academic year.

"I meet all the criteria," he said. "What do you think?"

Well, that was a bolt out of the blue! I hadn't considered doing anything other than carrying on as we were, however awful it was. Surely it would get better in time, and I wasn't unhappy, not really. Then I had a moment of panic, as I had only been teaching for less than a year, the minimum requirement was five years experience and there was no way I could teach Science. Was Richie thinking of leaving me behind?

"No, don't be stupid," he said, kissing me. "We'd have to see if you could get a visa, and if you could get work too, and obviously we wouldn't do it unless we'd both be happy, but … well … it would be an experience and it couldn't be much worse than this!"

In the end, we didn't go out at all that night. We talked, we researched, we talked some more and, by the time we went to bed, we had determined to at least find out if it would be possible. If our school would agree to the exchange, if I could get a work permit, if I was allowed to live with him … if, if, if. If all those questions were answered and it was a possibility, then he would apply and I would resign my post, as there was no chance of it being held open for me. It was a risk, but we were young and we felt as if our youth and energy were being stolen from us. We would give it a try.

After that, everything happened so quickly that even Richie, who was most logical person you could ever hope to meet, said that it seemed as if it were meant to happen. It was like watching a computer-generated sequence of a jigsaw being completed, each piece sliding effortlessly into place, with no hesitation, no false moves. By half term I had handed in my notice, and shortly after that, Richie received all the details of his new school, his flat, even some of his teaching commitments. We were going to

Ontario, to a town called Hamilton, and now that it was a reality, I couldn't wait.

We decided to have our leaving party a couple of weeks before the end of term. Even though we weren't due to fly out until the end of July, many of our teacher friends would be on their way to France or Spain or Italy as soon as the holiday started, and the last week of term was always busy. It was to be on the Saturday and we had booked the back room of The White Horse for the venue. It seemed fitting, given that our relationship had experienced its first faltering moments there, and of course the band was going to play. This would be my last gig with them for a year, and of course I was sad, but they had assured me I could step right back in as soon as we returned.

"A year isn't that long," said Olga, laughing and crying at once when I told her. "We'll probably still be playing most of the same songs!"

So, by the Friday, everything was more or less ready. Richie's flat – our flat, as it was by then – was still in disarray, with half-full storage boxes everywhere, but we had plenty of time to finish packing. The party was our priority, and we both had our tasks that evening. Mine was to go to The White Horse with Olga and put up the decorations and Richie's was to go into town. He had to visit the Indian restaurant providing the buffet, check that everything was in hand, then meet his parents at the station. He'd go with them in a taxi to their hotel and settle them in, before having a last drink with a friend who was leaving the country the next day and so would be unable to attend. We had a list of things to do taped to one of the kitchen units, and I got a strange, muddled feeling of excitement and panic every time I crossed something off.

Olga was an absolute star. She had told me to leave it all to her, saying that this would be her contribution to the party, and nothing I could say would change her mind, so I did, arriving at the pub completely empty-handed. She was already there, and had started arranging the tables so they formed a horseshoe around the dancing area. There were balloons and little arrangements of dried flowers in pots already in place, and boxes of other decorations by the stage.

Tears came to my eyes as I saw her there, working so hard to make everything right. She was my best friend and I was leaving her. Was I doing the right thing?

"Don't be daft," she said, when I had finished snuffling on her shoulder. "It's absolutely the right thing to be doing. I wish I was coming with you, the way things are here, and you'll be back before you know it, all refreshed and enthusiastic. You know I'm right."

I did know, but that didn't make it any easier, and it wasn't the last time I shed a few tears that evening, but the room looked brilliant by the time we had finished. It was almost unrecognisable from the fairly spartan back room we were used to, and Olga's eye for design had given it an ambience that was at once chic and cosy. It was all I could have asked for and more, and so I insisted on taking her into the bar for a drink before we left, even though we were both driving and it would have to be fruit juice. Richie would probably be quite late, and the flat was hardly welcoming, so I enjoyed an hour or so with her, just the two of us. There wouldn't be many more opportunities for this, and I wanted to make the most of it.

By the time I got home I was just about dead on my feet and ready for bed, but Richie still wasn't back and I wanted to tell him about the room and how wonderful it looked, so I ran a bath and had a lovely soak. I even nodded off for a few minutes, so I dried myself, put on my dressing gown and curled up on the sofa. He wouldn't be much longer now, after all, it was approaching midnight and most of the pubs in town stopped taking orders at 11pm. Any minute now, he'd be jumping out of a taxi at the end of the street and walking the couple of hundred yards down to the flat. I put on the television, but soon my eyes began to droop and I could not concentrate. I would just have a little snooze.

I was awoken, not that much later, by the sound of voices outside. This was unusual, as our street was a cul-de-sac and was generally very quiet, but I was still half-asleep and inclined to ignore it when there was a loud thumping on the door. I staggered across to the window and pulled the curtain aside, and I could see a figure crouched beside something on the pavement. I couldn't make out what it was, due to the low wall that marked our tiny patch of front garden, but there was someone else at the door, thumping and ringing the bell then standing back to look at the windows, so I hurried to the hall. Clearly something had happened outside and somebody was in need of help.

A young woman, ashen-faced, confronted me as I opened the door.

"Quick, call an ambulance, the police! There's a knife in his chest. My mobile's dead and Simon can't, he's … he's …"

From the front door I could see that somebody was on the ground, so I didn't wait to find out why Simon could not phone an ambulance, but rushed inside, found my phone and called for both an ambulance and the police. I was calm and collected and I was first aid trained, so I exchanged my dressing gown for a coat and went outside to help whilst we waited for the ambulance.

That was when two things became clear, and I don't know which came first or whether it all happened at once, but my life changed for ever in those few seconds, as I saw that the person bleeding on the ground was Richie and that he was certainly dead.

What happened after that is muddled and I don't care to try to remember it in detail. Apparently I tried to revive him and had to be pulled from his body when the police arrived. Apparently I was covered in blood – as was the unfortunate Simon, who couldn't bring himself to use his phone when he saw the state of his hands. When somebody is stabbed in the heart there is an awful lot of blood and they don't take long to die. I suppose it was meant to be a comfort to me that Richie would have lost consciousness quite quickly, but I couldn't get it out of my head that he died there alone, on the street. What would have gone through his head in whatever time he had? He would have been thinking of me, I know that, and of all we had, all we had to lose; it was all slipping away from him and he couldn't stop it.

'A random act of meaningless violence.' That's what one of the newspaper reports said, and the words 'random' and 'meaningless' were often used by people when they talked about it. I don't know whether it would have been easier to cope with if it had been otherwise – if somebody had hated him enough to want to kill him, or if he had died saving a child from a burning house – but it was very difficult to make any sense of it, especially as no-one was ever caught. There was no CCTV in our little street. The knife was a standard kitchen knife, the sort everyone has in their homes, unmarked, no prints, not even new. Its blade had been sharpened to a lethal point, but it was unremarkable in every other way. There was no motive. No motive at all. We went over and over it, both with the police and with his family, his friends, our friends, but there was nobody who would have wanted him dead, not even a disgruntled pupil, although quite a few of them were pulled in and interviewed.

The case was never closed, and the police assured me that they would revisit it as soon as any other evidence became available, but it never did. Richie was simply in the wrong place at the wrong time, although being right outside your own home should be safe enough. He just happened to be there at the same time as somebody who was clearly deranged. We will never know what led up to it, whether there was some kind of altercation, whether it could have been avoided if only he had handed over his wallet or his phone. I have had to learn to stop thinking about it as there are no answers and no satisfactory endings. Richie died. He didn't die of cancer, or in a road accident, or from some previously undetected heart condition. He didn't die of anything that we might have predicted, if we had ever had such a conversation, but he was stabbed. It was random and meaningless, but there was nothing anyone could do about that.

So, people rallied round to do all the things that could be done. Practical things. I was in no condition to deal with the multiplicity of difficulties arising from Richie's death, but my friends resolved the issues of the tenancy, my job – everything that had been put in place to secure our new future and now needed to be unpicked. Olga was particularly supportive, but Nat was there too, although he was in almost as bad a state as I was, and others. For weeks I was hardly ever alone, and the flat was returned to some semblance of order. Many of Richie's possessions were taken away by his heartbroken family and mine were unpacked. The boxes disappeared, food appeared in the cupboards, and I functioned at some level in the weeks leading up to the funeral, although I have little memory of that time now.

Obviously the circumstances of Richie's death meant that the funeral was delayed. There was an inquest, with the predictable outcome of unlawful killing, but that was a long time later, and at least his body was released in late August. That was how we came to be saying goodbye to him on a bright, sunny morning, with everyone in bright, sunny clothes, as he would have wanted. I don't remember ever having had a 'my funeral' conversation with him, but there were plenty of people who seemed to know what his thoughts would be, if he were here to give them, and I had neither the energy nor inclination to express an opinion. I didn't even help choose the music, although that was something we had talked about a lot, as it was simply too painful. I didn't see the point in exposing everybody's nerve endings in this way, but I endured it when they played Nirvana's 'All Apologies' and something by The Smiths. I don't know what it was. These were from the soundtrack of Richie's youth, a time I hadn't shared, and now we wouldn't be sharing any more time and there would be no more music in my life.

There were so many people at the funeral that they had to relay it via speakers to the crowd outside and reserve seats inside the chapel for those who knew him best. There must have been a hundred students outside, sitting on the grass, and if it hadn't been for the fact that many were in tears and others were comforting them you might have thought that a mini-festival was being held in the grounds of the municipal crematorium. Then there were his family, his colleagues, his many, many friends, some of whom would have been at the party that never took place, and were now here together in quite a different mood. And then there was me. I was right at the front, they insisted on that, but I could take no solace from Nat's supportive arm, from the kind words of all the people who stood up to say what a great person he'd been, or to read poems, or to tell funny little anecdotes about things he had done. I was stony-faced, untouchable, detached and hiding behind my own little wall.

That was until Olga and Tim stood up and walked to the front. Tim was carrying his acoustic guitar, and a deeper hush fell upon the packed congregation.

"I hadn't known Richie for long," said Olga, "but I do know Amy." She glanced over at me, and I saw her take a deep breath. "I know that Richie made Amy as happy as she has ever been, and that tells me all I need to know. This song is for Richie, but it's also for Amy, to let her know that we will all be here for her, for as long as she needs us."

It was Bob Dylan. It was 'Knockin' on Heaven's Door', the same song that I had sung all those months ago, when Richie was still a question mark in my mind and life stretched out before me, full of opportunity. It was not the same version I'd sung, as Olga's voice was stronger and huskier than mine and it was more like Dylan's own rendition. But it broke down my defences all the same, dismantled my wall, brick by brick, until I was completely exposed and my grief and anger and despair flooded out in one long, animal-like howl.

***

So now it's evening I suppose. It has been dark for a while, and I've eaten a little soup and cried quite a lot. If I carry on like this I will have no strength, no reserves to deal with Greg when he comes. Or, if he doesn't come, if I have to spend days or even weeks here, what state will I be in, if I am ever rescued? I want to be able to throw myself back into life if I get the chance, not spend more precious months in recovery, in some kind of facility or in the flat again, the threat coming from the outside world in general rather than Greg. Surely there is more to me than this?

I stand up and walk to the door, pull the desk away, and listen hard, my ear against the wood. There is nothing, not the tiniest sound to indicate that anyone else is here, but I shout and bang on the door with my fists. Help! Help! Somebody, please help me! I pick up the chair and heave it against the door, but it only bounces off, narrowly avoiding my head before clattering to the floor. There is a long scrape on the green paintwork now, but hardly a dent. This is a solid wood door, not some flimsy panelled thing that the hero in a film could punch his way through. You would shatter your knuckles before you punched any kind of hole in this door, but I feel better all the same. Come on girl, show your spirit! Don't let him win! Make Nat proud of you, so you are all in one piece when he comes.

Unbelievably, I smile a little. That's what I will do. When all this is over, I will take Nat on holiday. I don't care how much it costs, I will get the money from somewhere. Maybe Mum and Dad will lend me some, when they find out what I've been through and what Nat did to help. We will go somewhere peaceful and chill out, or no, maybe not. Maybe we'll go to New York, or Mexico City! Yes, that's it! We will go somewhere exciting, and I will not be scared, as nothing could be as scary as this and, probably, I will never be scared of anything again if only I come out the other side.

I lie back on the bed and imagine this holiday. I think about walking down the gangway of a plane with Nat behind me, feeling the blast of heat from the tarmac, hearing the endless chirp of the crickets, but then I am gripped by sadness. What am I doing? I am fantasising about a holiday with Nat, but it is Richie I want to be with. Somehow, Greg has even stolen my grief. He didn't take Richie away from me, we know that, but I have not been able to deal normally with his death because of this constant threat to my safety. So no, there will be no celebrations if I am saved. I will not go on holiday. I will find a way to lead some kind of normal life that doesn't have Richie in it, as that is what he would want, but I'm not ready to feel happy yet and I don't really want to.

***

I've no idea what happened next. Obviously the service continued, but I had to be taken outside, with all the eyes of the assembled crowd watching as Nat helped me down the path and to his car, and the next thing I can remember in any detail is being back at the flat and a doctor shining a light into my eyes.

I only took the tablets for about three months. I've absolutely nothing against medication, and it did help me get through the darkest times, but I wasn't depressed, not in the clinical sense of the word. I was bereaved, and the only way to recover from that is to let time do its work and slowly, carefully, force yourself back into the land of the living. So that's what I did, with an enormous amount of support, and by New Year I was beginning to lead some kind of a life again. Christmas had been terrible, of course, and New Year itself, as I couldn't help remembering all the happy times we'd had last year and that we'd never got to spend Christmas Day together. Still, the human spirit is unbelievably robust and I taught my first class for nearly six months at the start of the new term. Somebody said it would be like getting back onto a bike, and that turned out to be true. I was a bit wobbly, but I was fine.

Christmas Eve

Somehow, it is morning again. I had a terrible night, waking with a jolt I don't know how many times, thinking I could hear somebody at the door. I had a horrible dream in which Richie and I were on a beach, somewhere idyllic, and then he got up and said he was going for a swim, so I watched him, watched the white of his body dive dolphin-like through the waves, then tracked the arch of his arms, graceful in a lazy crawl until I could see him no more. I was not worried. In my dream I knew he was a strong swimmer, so I dozed in the sun until his shadow fell on my face and he lay down beside me, wet and salty, and we kissed long and hard, his arms pulling me closer and our legs beginning to entwine. Then something happened, and I realised, suddenly, it was not Richie I was kissing, but Nat, but I told myself not to worry, Richie wouldn't mind, and we kissed some more until I shook myself awake, gasping with guilt and regret.

I'm no psychologist, but that dream does not take a lot of interpretation. I went to sleep feeling guilty about planning a holiday with Nat, and my dream was exploring that guilt, but I could not put the idea of Nat kissing me out of my mind. It was only the product of my imagination, but is there some ambiguity in my feelings for Nat? There is a huge amount of gratitude, a huge amount of dependence on his support, but there is also that feeling of being suffocated from time to time. Poor Nat, I can't imagine how hurt he would be if he knew it, but I could never live with him, even as a friend, and it was so difficult to deal with when the issue arose.

***

It was Olga who suggested that we should get a place together. She said it must be difficult living in the space I had shared with Richie, especially as it had been his flat, and there was some truth in that. Most of the furniture had been his, and I hadn't lived there long enough to really make it my own before we got rid of a lot of stuff in preparation for the move to Canada. A teacher called Jack had been going to live there as part of the exchange, and we'd had to de-personalise it as much as we could. So now it was a sad place really, with most of Richie's things gone and aching spaces where they used to be. Olga was right. It was time for a move, and her lease was coming to an end in six months so she would have to find somewhere else. I didn't know at the time, as I had been so wrapped up in my own problems, but she had been having a painful and secret fling with Anton's brother, who had some sort of complicated on-off relationship with someone else, and it had all ended messily. However, Olga was too concerned about me to talk about her own problems. What was a dent to her self-esteem compared to what I had been through?

So we were looking for a place. Not that actively, as it was still some time before we could move in, but I was beginning to feel quite excited about it. OK it was no substitute for what I'd lost, but I would not even consider another relationship, and if it made sense to share, who better to share with than Olga, the best friend a girl could ever have?

I'm not sure whether I'd actually said anything to Nat about it. I suppose I hadn't, given what happened. He had been incredibly kind, phoning almost every day, popping round with a takeaway meal if he thought I sounded low, sorting out so many things. He was like my big brother, or even my dad, although the extent of my own parents' support was to say that it all may turn out for the best, as my career could only have suffered from taking a year's break. No surprise then, that I chose not to see a lot of them from that point.

Still, it was more than a surprise, it was a shock, when he came round to the flat one evening with a serious look on his face.

"There's something I want to discuss with you," he said, handing me a bottle of red, "and I think we should do it over a drink."

I had absolutely no idea what he was going to say, although I did wonder if he'd met someone and was worried about telling me that he would have less time to spend with me. I wouldn't have minded about that, as there was nothing I wanted more than for him to find a partner. Although he could never be the man for me, even if I'd met him before Richie, there was no doubt that he would make a wonderful, caring boyfriend for somebody, and it was strange that it never seemed to happen for him. Richie used to say that it showed how superficial people were.

"They don't see the real Nat," he once said. "They can't see what shines through. It's a bloody travesty."

So, there we were, sitting somewhat formally on the sofa, with glasses of wine on the coffee table in front of us, the TV off and something in the air. I couldn't put my finger on what it was, but it was there.

"The thing is, my Great Aunt Ellen has died," Nat said. I started to say something about being sorry, as you do, but he stopped me. "No, don't worry, it's OK. She was in her nineties, completely away with the fairies for the last couple of years. She's been in a home for some years, and she has – had – a house in Camden that was rented out to pay the fees. I had to sort it all out when she started to lose the plot. Anyway, you don't need to know about all that. The thing is, she looked after me when my grandparents got too old and nobody else could be bothered, and we became very close. She didn't have any children of her own, and, well, she's left me the house."

I really wasn't sure what to say. Why was he telling me this? Was it because he was sad really, but didn't know how to express it? As if reading my thoughts, he took a swig of his wine, topped it up again and continued.

"Obviously there are tenants in there at the moment, but we've always operated short-term leases and I'll be in a position to sell it within months. It might even sell with the tenants in place. Anyway, I was thinking about buying somewhere round here, and I thought why not get somewhere I could convert into two flats?" He looked across at me, as if for confirmation, so I nodded and smiled.

"Sounds great," I said. "I imagine you'd get something pretty good round here if the house is in Camden. You could convert them to a really high standard, live in one yourself ..."

"... And you could live in the other!" he said. "Exactly! It's the perfect solution. I wouldn't charge you the commercial rent, obviously, and you could have complete control over the décor, the fittings, all that. I'd always be there for you, but you'd be completely independent."

There was an uncomfortable silence. I had been going to say that he could sell the other flat. It hadn't even entered my mind that I could live in it. I was already seeing myself ensconced with Olga, in a flat which represented our different but complementary personalities, a flat that was vibrant and homely, with Olga's big, squashy sofa in the centre and the walls lined with our books and music. I didn't want to live by myself, however beautiful the flat. I was still young, and I was looking forward to the fun and laughter, the queuing for the bathroom, the coming home to find someone had cooked dinner or baked a cake.

"Oh, Nat, that's so kind, so thoughtful of you to include me in your plans. Another time it would have been perfect, but I'm going to move in with Olga for a while. We're looking for somewhere at the moment, as she's got to leave her place and I want the company. She's my best friend, and we've lived together before. But thanks, thanks so much for thinking of me!"

That wasn't all I said. I rambled on about what a good idea it was, how he should go ahead and do it anyway, but he left shortly afterwards and I don't know what he did with the money from the house. Certainly he didn't use it to convert any flats. That just shows the kind of person he is. The only reason he had for doing it was to provide me with a comfortable and safe place to live, and when I rejected that he lost interest. Poor Nat. He was obviously disappointed, but it didn't affect anything. He was just as kind, just as thoughtful, in the weeks and months that followed and thank goodness for that.

So, I was taking my first tentative steps towards repairing my life. Obviously I was still very fragile, and there were times when the enormity of it all overwhelmed me or when I wondered whether it was worth carrying on, but there was always someone there to pick up the pieces. I would go round to Olga's, or Nat would come round to mine. There would be tears, there would be anger at the pointless stupidity of it all, hours of 'if only' conversations in which they would listen whilst I berated myself for not preventing it in some way. Then they would help me to understand that I couldn't have, that life and death really are randomly cruel sometimes, and that would work for a while, until the next low point.

Slowly, the gaps between these episodes of despair became longer and I became stronger. I got up on stage with Olga in March, not to sing alone, but it was a first step, and our flat-hunting became more serious. I had only a short notice period on my lease, as Nat thought that was best when he renegotiated it for me, but Olga had to be out by the end of June. There was never a day that passed without Richie popping into my mind, never a morning without the ache of realisation that he wasn't there, but there were days when I could be almost normal, at least when I wasn't alone. I spent more and more time at Olga's flat, poring over the property sites on her laptop whilst she rustled up a pasta dish in that way that she had, making something tasty from an apparently unpromising selection of sad-looking vegetables.

When Nat made his regular calls to ask how I was, I could quite honestly tell him that I was fine. I hoped that he, too, would be able to start building up more of a social life. I was only too aware that I was not the only one who had been bereaved on that terrible night, and sometimes I felt guilty that he had done all the supporting whilst he must have needed support too. But I could not fill that gap for him. He had been Richie's friend, not mine, and I could not replace Richie. That's what I told myself as I hung up one evening, knowing that Olga was looking across at me with that 'not him again' look on her face, and I felt terrible about the slightly sinking feeling I would get when I saw his number on the display. What a heartless, ungrateful person I was, to feel this way when he had been so kind, so supportive. I would never have said anything to him, but I did cut him short from time to time.

It was just as well that we never fell out about it, that he didn't give up on me as, completely out of the blue, Greg started to contact me again. I couldn't believe it was happening, but there it was, a card in my pigeonhole at school. The address was printed on a label and the envelope was plain and white, so I didn't think anything of it as I tore it open, but the elaborate heart on the front made my heart pound and I opened it with shaking hands. The inside was printed too, a piece of paper glued beneath the message, so the whole thing read:

> To the one I love
> I have missed you so much and have been thinking of you in your time of unhappiness. Maybe I can help you to move on?
> Your friend always

I don't know how long I stood there, with the card in my hand, reading it over and over again. How could this be? Obviously he would have known about Richie's death – it had been in all the papers and on the local news – but why wait this long to make contact? If I thought about him at all, which was very rarely by then, I assumed he had forgotten all about me, found someone else. It was incredible, but it seemed he had been thinking about me all this time, watching and waiting for the time he could step into Richie's shoes. I dropped the card, ran to the toilets, and was violently sick. This could not be true.

But it was true, and it was only the start of it. To begin with, I was strong, and I threw away any post with printed labels, or gave them to Olga to open. The staff at reception were given instructions to reject any flowers delivered for me, and there were strict procedures about divulging any staff email addresses in place by that time, so I thought I could manage it. I didn't even tell Nat, as I was worried about him charging round to Greg's house and making a scene. Richie had told me how brilliant he had been the first time, keeping the situation calm when Greg denied it all at first, making it possible for it all to seem like a misunderstanding, but I doubted it would be the same now. He was very protective of me, and I couldn't predict what might happen.

I suppose it was no surprise that I couldn't keep it up. It was less than a year after I had suffered a major trauma and I began to dread going into school for fear of what I might find there. I couldn't talk to my colleagues about it as it seemed so ridiculous. Who was I to have a stalker? Was I claiming to be some kind of a celebrity? Of course I know now that there were many, many people in school who would have listened sympathetically and offered me support. I doubt that anyone would have thought I was being self-obsessed or any of the other things I worried about, but hindsight is a wonderful thing and that is what I thought at the time. I thought they would talk about me behind my back, or make light of it in that way that teachers do when there is something serious to worry about. I couldn't bear the thought of being the subject of staffroom gossip, so I told the reception staff a story about an ex-boyfriend who was trying to win me back. I laughed and said it wasn't anything serious, but could they just send any flowers away, and keep it to themselves? They may have told people, I don't know. It wasn't long before flowers were the least of my problems.

***

Today, I have eaten some granola with a little milk, and heated some water in the microwave to make tea. I had to make up the milk from powder, and it's not the best option for tea, but now I feel fortified and a little stronger. It is hard to imagine that a third day will pass with no contact, so I turn my thoughts to the door. There has to be a solution.

I close my eyes, and let my mind travel around the room. There is something there, some little thought that won't quite come to the surface, so I get up and pace up and down. There's the wardrobe; only clothes and bedding in there. There's the fridge-freezer; only food in there. There's the little cupboard; nothing substantial in there. There's the bed. Nothing there, but what is it made of? It's made of wood, and it's new, and it's almost certainly self-assembly. Somebody brought it up here in pieces, so … That's it! If it has been put together, the chances are it can be taken apart. I am gripped by a great rush of excitement. This could be the answer.

But there is a problem with this bed. Not only is it fixed to the floor, but most of the sections are held in place by metal fittings with a hexagonal head. Some kind of Allen key will have been provided in the pack, and Greg is not stupid enough to have left it behind. I would have found it by now if he had. However, I pull the mattress onto the floor, and I can see that some of the slats are not fixed at both ends, and that they are held in place with screws. Nothing complicated, not even cross-head, just normal screws. If I could only find some way to loosen those screws, I could remove some of the slats and use them. I don't know how yet, but I will think of something, if I can get them off.

I sit there for quite a while, pondering. Sometimes the answer to a problem will come to me if I do that, but not this time, so I try pulling one of the slats, jiggling it around, tapping it from underneath with my shoe, but it does not loosen. Surely there must be a way.

It is quite a while later that I remember my little coin. It is so tiny, that it might just fit into the grooves in the screw heads, so I find it in the drawer and take it across to the bed. Some of the screws are tight, and flush with the wood, but some are not. Greg's craftsmanship seems to have been a bit sloppy, or maybe he was in a hurry when he got to this part of the assembly, but this could work to my advantage as several of the screws stand proud of the wood and are not completely tight.

I take my little coin and try it in one of the promising screws, and yes, it fits. It will only work on those that are already a little loose, but I persevere, until I have two slats and four screws there on the floor in front of me. Quickly, I drag the mattress back onto the bed frame and arrange the bedding. If Greg were to arrive now the game would be up, so I hide the slats and the screws in the wardrobe and lie back on the bed. My fingers are sore from twisting the coin, and I am sweating from the exertion, but there is no way I'm going back into the shower, so I try to relax. I need a few minutes to think clearly.

***

Dreams are funny things, aren't they? I can remember no nightmares after Richie was killed, no horrific visions of dark figures approaching, wielding knives. I had plenty of dreams in which Richie explained to me, in apparently reasonable terms, how he was able to continue talking to me despite being dead, and quite a lot of dreams in which he wasn't dead at all, but they were not scary. He would just be there, his usual self, often in a quite mundane context, and sometimes, if my dream self remembered that he was supposed to be dead, he would tell me that it had all been a mistake. This would provoke a huge wave of happiness and relief that would only dissipate as I awoke, and this was hard at first, but after a while, there could be something approaching comfort in waking up and remembering what I had dreamed.

I'd had a particularly vivid dream on the morning the next stage started. That's probably why I remember it so well. Richie and I had been in the staffroom together, and I was explaining to colleagues that he hadn't died really and now he was back to take up his post again. It was only a brief snippet, but Richie himself was very clear, even to the point of wearing his school suit – a shiny blue one that had seen better days, with an open-necked shirt. The image kept popping into my mind as I made my breakfast, so I went through into the lounge to watch TV whilst I ate. It wasn't that I didn't want to think about Richie, I still thought about him all the time, but this dream was making me sad.

I heard the letterbox rattle as I put my plate and mug on the coffee table. It was unlikely there would be anything exciting in the post, but I went to fetch it anyway as it might help to take my mind off that recurring image of Richie in the staffroom. There was one brown envelope on the mat. My name and address were on a printed label, but I didn't think anything of that. This looked like an official communication, although I suppose, if I had been thinking clearly, I would have remarked on the fact that it was stamped rather than franked. Anyway, I started to open it as I walked back to the lounge, and put the contents on the coffee table whilst I turned on the TV. Sitting down, I picked up the single, folded sheet of paper and opened it out, and it is just as well I hadn't picked up my coffee, or I would quite probably have tipped it all over myself.

Dear Amy,

I understand how difficult it must be for you to receive my gifts at your workplace. None of us likes our private lives to be on display, and you have suffered enough of that in the past few months. That is why I have decided to stop communicating with you at school but to use your home address instead. This way it will be just between ourselves, and our relationship will be able to develop normally.

I must say that I have huge admiration for the way you have picked up the pieces of your life. You often seem to be smiling these days, and it was lovely to see you back on stage. Now I can't wait for your next appearance – will there be a solo this time?

I'll finish now. I just thought it was important to let you know that I do understand why you didn't feel able to receive anything at school and I'm not at all offended! I know you would never want to upset me, so you can put your mind at rest on that score.
Bye for now, and I'll be in touch again soon,
Your friend

I was stunned. Assaulted by waves of conflicting emotions: anger, fear, disbelief. I think I may even have laughed out loud. What on earth was he thinking? How could he possibly believe that our relationship – which did not even exist – could 'develop normally' through the medium of unsolicited letters and gifts? Did he really think that I had been worrying about upsetting him? Even more concerning were the remarks about how happy I appeared to be and about seeing me sing. There had been no sign of him at the gig, and I had not seen his car outside school since Richie and Nat warned him off. That meant he was somehow watching me in secret, and that was very scary indeed.

I grabbed my mobile, and it was Nat that I called. I had been seeing much more of Olga recently, but Nat understood about all this. He had been there from the start and I knew he would take it seriously. Of course I had told Olga about what had happened before Richie died, but her response had been that we had been much too soft and, if she'd known, she would have got some friends to hold him down whilst she kicked him where it would hurt the most. She had been joking, but it wasn't the kind of response I was looking for now, with the letter lying on the table in front of me. I wanted someone who was calm, sensible and practical, and Nat was all of those things and more.

Of course he dropped everything and came round straight away, and we spent ages analysing the letter, looking for clues. What were his intentions? Could he really be that deluded? We decided not to confront him, at least not for the moment, as he had stopped signing his name and there was no actual proof that he was involved. Nat said this demonstrated that he was not completely mad, as he would have seen no reason to withhold his name if that were the case, and that meant we would have to tread more carefully. He told me not to worry, then took my laptop and showed me a security website.

"I deal with these people at work, and they're good," he said. "Plus, I can get a discount. All we need is a security light that comes on if anyone approaches the door, and a couple of these little cameras that link up to your laptop. You will be able to look at the footage every day when you get home, and see who has been to your door. We can make one of them look outwards, to the street, in case he is standing there watching."

The thought of Greg standing there watching my flat made me shiver, but I agreed to everything Nat said. He didn't even want any money in advance, and then he took me out for a late lunch before dropping me off again, right at my door. He wouldn't even hear of me walking down the street by myself and made me promise to take the car everywhere for the time being.

"Just until we get the cameras in place," he said. "I'll feel more comfortable then."

I spent the next few days feeling anxious and jittery. Olga and I had planned to go out that night, and it would have been much more sensible to have gone, to have put it all behind me and had a good time, but I was queasy and my head was thumping, so I cried off. I made it to band practice the next day, and that gave me a few hours of respite, but I had a terrible sinking feeling as I drove home.

As if to confirm all my fears, there was a bouquet of flowers on the doorstep. I could hardly leave them there, it would look as if the flat were empty and that could attract trouble so I picked them up, gingerly, as if a bomb or a venomous snake might be hiding between the blooms. There was no snake, only a small card. Nothing was written on it, just a rather badly-drawn heart, but that was worse if anything. I took the flowers inside and spent five minutes cutting them into tiny segments and cramming the whole lot into the bin. It was far too full really, but I would have had to go out to the bulk bins at the back of the flat, and that felt unsafe. This was the first time I had felt this way, even in the aftermath of Richie's murder, so I phoned Nat and asked him to order an extra camera for the back. That would do the trick.

So, by the end of that week, there were cameras trained on both the entrances to my flat, and one on the area of the street beyond the front gate. Nat fitted it all himself, as he said it would save me a fortune, and then he showed me how to log into the system and replay the footage. I have no idea how it all worked, and haven't to this day, but it was not difficult to operate once it was all installed. The cameras would only record any significant movement, so I did not have to scan hours and hours of footage in which nothing happened, but as we flicked through on the first evening, it was a surprise to find out how many of the neighbourhood cats considered my flat to be in their territory.

Two or three weeks passed and I developed a routine. The minute I was inside the flat I would check the post for any of Greg's cards or letters, any odd little gifts he had ordered from online providers, and then I would log on and check the security footage. I could not relax until I had done this, although it only proved what we had suspected from the start: Greg was clearly unbalanced, but he was still lucid enough never to approach the flat himself and never to stand anywhere within the range of the cameras. He used the postal service, and online services that would not divulge the details of their clients. We had enough information to know what he was doing, but not enough to do anything about it.

Nat said the next thing we should do was to cut off Greg's oxygen supply. Not literally, although there were times when I wouldn't have argued a lot about that, but in terms of information. It was time to block him on Facebook and other social media sites, and I should take the opportunity to reduce the number of friends I had.

"It's not that they are a risk in themselves," he said. "It's just that you can't control what they do. If they have accepted friend requests from Greg, that gives him access to some of your posts. It won't be for long, but you need to be quite drastic and cull everyone you don't know very well."

So, that's what I did. I posted a vague explanation then unfriended the vast majority of my contacts, leaving a small group of the people I knew best. I sent a different message to them, via email, asking them to block Greg if he was already a friend, and never to accept him if he was not. Most people replied quickly, asking if I was alright and promising their support, but only three had Greg as a friend, so it seemed that he preferred the personal approach to online snooping anyway.

I did feel better though. It was good to know that my posts were not winging their way to a group of people who were virtual strangers. I don't know why I had been so careless in the old days before all this started, but I was a changed person now. I rarely posted anything, and used my account to keep track of my friends' much more exciting lives, rather than to record my own.

I can't remember what happened next. Whether it was Olga texting to say she had found the perfect flat for us or the first of the nasty letters. It doesn't really matter, as I know I had already begun to doubt the wisdom of moving in with her. Looking back, this is hard to justify, but I suppose it demonstrates the siege mentality I was already beginning to develop. Surely there would have been safety in numbers? Surely Greg would have been put off by the close proximity of another person? That may well have been true, and it is possible that it all would have stopped if I had taken a different path, but at the time, I could not see how it would work.

For a start, I could not see Olga agreeing to the level of security upon which I now depended. She was characteristically cavalier about the whole thing – or maybe I played it down when I was with her, that is possible – and I could just imagine her response to the idea of multiple cameras trained on every visitor who came to the flat. She is an extremely sociable person, and the idea that everyone she invited back would be recorded as they arrived and left would have horrified her.

Then there was the issue of Nat. I completely relied on him, in more ways than one, in a very different way to how I relied on Olga, but they really didn't get on. There hadn't been any kind of conflict, but Olga can never disguise her feelings very well, and the way she rolled her eyes when I mentioned something he had said spoke volumes.

"Oh, well, if Nat says it's true I suppose it must be," she would say. I didn't like to think that the two people I was closest to did not like each other, but there was no getting away from it. Nat is usually an extremely charming person, and has a way of putting people at ease when he meets them. You can see them relaxing, smiling, as he does instinctively what any social skills manual would advise. He looks straight at you, right into your eyes, and he always seems to know the right questions to ask, how much physical contact to make, all that kind of thing. Apart from with Olga. Richie and I had been going out for a few weeks before they met at a party, and I must have talked about her and how lovely she was, but they simply didn't hit it off and I could see Nat didn't warm to her effusiveness any more than she warmed to his charm.

"Sorry, but I found him superficial," she told me in the kitchen, as we searched for clean glasses. I said it was a very brief meeting to be making a judgement like that, and she laughed and said she supposed it was, but even though they were regularly thrown together by my relationship with Richie, their own relationship developed no further. They were polite and guarded when they met, and although Olga was much more open about her feelings than Nat was – he wouldn't have wanted to hurt me – I'm sure they were mutual.

That being the case, how could Nat continue to oversee my security system in a completely different flat, with Olga around? It wasn't only the cameras, there were bits and pieces inside too. I don't know what they were, something to boost the signal I think he said, and all this would have to be dismantled and put back again in the new flat. Would Olga agree to this? Would she cope with Nat popping round almost daily, to take a quick look at the footage or check everything was working? Somehow I couldn't see it, and now that Olga had a prospective flat for me to view, I would have to stop pushing this issue to one side and confront it.

I think that conversation was one of the most difficult I have ever had. With the exception of telling people about what had happened to Richie, it may have been one of the saddest too. I had already alerted Olga to the fact that there was a problem, but this was not something to say in a text or over the phone, so I told her I was coming round to discuss it, and winced at the surprise in her voice.

"What's the matter? Has something happened?"

"No, not as such, but there are issues. Look, can we talk about it when I come?" I said. It was already obvious that this was going to be hard, but it had to be done, and I drove round to hers with my stomach churning away and my eyes pricking with tears. This was all Greg's fault! If it wasn't for him, I'd be packing my stuff into boxes, looking forward to a new phase of my life, despite the sadness that was always there. Why did he have to do it? Why couldn't he just go away?

By the time I got there, I had worked myself up into a state and I fell into her arms and sobbed. She held me and comforted me, gradually calmed me down and teased it out of me, but it was all downhill from that point. She simply could not see why the new flat, in a different part of town, wasn't the solution to the problem. She thought Greg would give up if I ignored him for long enough, but I knew that stalkers can carry on their campaigns for years, resolutely ignoring any evidence that does not fit in with their vision of the so-called relationship with their victim. I had read enough to know that, and I had also read enough to know that the police should be involved, but that was something we had not done.

"Why not, then?" demanded Olga. "If this thing is so bad that you can't move in with me, that you have to be holed up in your flat with cameras trained on you day and night, why haven't you been to the police?"

I explained about the lack of evidence. I avoided saying anything about Nat, but he was of the opinion that we needed more before the police would act. He was still hoping that Greg would give himself away, approach the flat or leave some other kind of evidence behind and then we would go to the police straight away. Of course we would.

Olga was not convinced, and she was angry and frustrated. She had spent months looking for a two-bedroom flat, and now, when her lease was running out, she had to start all over again. Added to that, she had been looking forward to us living together as I had, and she was disappointed, rejected.

"It's like you're saying I can't support you," she said, her voice rising. "What is this thing with Nat? Why has he become so important? You're not …?"

"No, of course I'm not," I cried. "How could you say such a thing? Richie hasn't even been dead for a year and I doubt I'll ever love anyone else, certainly not Nat. It's just that he keeps me safe, Olga, can't you see that? I'd love to live with you, but there would be no point if I didn't feel safe, would there? Maybe when this is all over ..."

"Yeah, maybe," she said, but I could see that it was time to go. Nothing I could say would make her understand how difficult it was to live with something like this. I'm sure I would have been the same if had been the other way round. Why don't you just do this? Why don't you just do that? It all looks so simple until it's you in that situation, and then the world seems like a very different place and nothing is simple, not even going out to get a pint of milk. Nothing is simple at all.

I drove home in tears, let myself in and phoned Nat. Although it was getting late by then, and I had done no preparation for the next day, he insisted on coming round with a bottle of red. A couple of glasses of that, together with his calm and logical approach, helped me to feel better. I agreed to call in sick the next day, and he would take a day's leave so we could work out a plan.

"I'm not having you become a victim," he said, although I already felt like exactly that. "Tomorrow is the start of our fight back. We are going to beat this, and you are going to get your life back!"

I was still tearful as he let himself out and I double-locked the door after him and slid the bolts into place. This was another of Nat's ideas, and it would certainly have taken more strength than I imagine Greg had to force his way through, but I can't say that I felt secure that night. I tried to concentrate on Nat's words, we were going to beat this, but what I was feeling was an overwhelming sense of loss, with Olga at the centre of it, and it would not go away.

***

So now I am very clear about what I'm missing. Locks and bolts that I can pull across from this side and they will stop the door opening even when it is unlocked from the other side. Obviously I can't have them, not in the same way as I had them at the flat, but I have the slats and I have the screws. I go to the wardrobe, take one of the slats from its hiding place under the spare bedding and carry it across to the door, holding it flat against the wood. If I could screw one end into the door frame and one into the door, surely that would provide some protection, especially if I fix one at the top and one at the bottom.

Suddenly, I am excited. This could really work, it could keep him out, and then he might draw attention to himself. Somebody might hear him crashing against the door and call the police. In any case, if it keeps him on one side of the door and me on the other, that is all I can ask for, at least for a while, so I fetch the screws and the coin and try to put my plan into action.

Some time later, I sit on the floor, my fingers sore and bleeding in places and only one screw in place. The door is made of extremely hard wood, and it is virtually impossible to make any impression with only the coin to exert any force. The frame is easier, but even that has been very hard work and the screw is not as tight as it should be. So now what do I do? There is no point in even starting the second slat if I can't solve the problem of the first, and I cry with the frustration of it. All I need is a couple of basic tools, a screwdriver, and maybe one of those things with a handle and a sharp spike. I don't know what it is called, but Dad had one in his tool box, and I can see him now, marking a cross with a pencil then pushing the spike into the wood, moving it around with a small, circular movement so the screw would have something on which to grip.

Of course! Why didn't I think of it before? I have my tacks, so I get one of them and take off my shoe so I can tap it into place. It makes a terrific noise, and the tack flies off in all directions over and over again, but I retrieve it each time and keep on tapping until, at last, it is sticking out of the wood. Then I have to knock it out again, with sideways movements so I can swing the slat across, post the screw through and into the little hole left by the tack. It is not easy, and there are several false starts, but eventually the second screw is about halfway in and the slat is in place. I cannot do any more, as my hands are too sore.

***

It is so hard to unpick everything. Sometimes it really is like a nightmare – not in the clichéd sense of it being terrifying, although that is true too, but in the way it has all become muddled in my head. Obviously there is a narrative thread, and one thing followed on from another, but I find it hard to see it. Still, even with this episodic memory, I think the first nasty letter must have come then, or soon after. It can't have been before I told Olga about the flat, as I doubt I would have been in a fit state to have driven over there if I had already received it. Outwardly, it looked no different from the others, so I opened it with a sigh and prepared to file it away in the folder Nat had suggested I keep. There was little hope that it would contain any evidence, or that Greg would have been stupid enough to sign it, but I had to read each one just in case.

Dear Amy,

I must confess to becoming a little irritated. I have been nothing but polite, thoughtful and caring, yet you repay me with silence. What have I done to deserve this? It would not take much of your precious time to give me some indication that you have enjoyed my gifts, after all. I have never seen you wear the silk scarf, I have never seen my cards displayed on your windowsill, and I wonder if you ever wear the silver locket? I took ages choosing that. You could at least have put the novelty air-freshener in your car where I would be sure to see it, but no, nothing. How could you be so unappreciative when I have tried so hard to please you?

I was quite prepared to carry on as we were for as long as it took, but now I am having to reconsider. You and I both know that we will be together in the end, and that this period is something we will look back on and laugh about one day, but come on! The joy of the chase is only a joy if the quarry is caught, and you my love, are my quarry.

I am sorry if this upsets you, but my feelings cannot be toyed with for ever.
Your devoted admirer

Fortunately, I was already sitting down when I read it, and I dropped the letter to the floor as if it were on fire. This was a real change from the cheery little notes I had received so far, and although they had been bad enough, there had been no hint of menace. I phoned Nat and told him there would be no more waiting to collect that significant piece of evidence. I was going to the police, now, today, and although he was at work he dropped everything and came to pick me up.

"We are in this together," he said, "and you are in such a state you might forget things."

This was true. Although it had shocked me into action, the letter had also completely thrown me. I had known that Greg was living in a world of his own invention, but I did not like the petulant tone nor the use of the word 'quarry'. This indicated something more sinister, more twisted, than I thought we were dealing with, and I was shaking from head to foot as we drove to the police station.

It was hours before we emerged again, calmer if not completely reassured. The police already knew about Greg, as I'd had to tell them about him when Richie was killed. I had never really thought he would be involved, and he had a very strong alibi, with CCTV footage of him and his parents entering and leaving a pizza restaurant and neighbours seeing them all arrive home at about 11 o'clock. There was the theoretical possibility that he had then driven back into town, waited for Richie outside the flat, killed him and returned home, but at least one of his neighbours was up until late and said she would have heard the car if he had gone out again. And then there were his parents, of course. They insisted that they had watched

TV with a hot drink until about midnight, and that Greg had been there with them throughout, and I for one doubted that they would have been very good liars.

So, Greg was not a suspect, but the police were aware that he had been pestering me, and that file was eventually located when Nat explained why we had come. Two different people saw us, took down the same information, examined the letters and the carrier bag of unwanted gifts, and then we had to wait for what seemed like hours before we were called back in.

"Right, well," said the detective, "it's not easy when there is no actual evidence to link these materials to Mr Payne, but we will have a quiet word with him. That will almost certainly be enough, and you have done the right thing. I know you dealt with it yourself before, but that was actually a very high-risk strategy and could have put yourself and others in danger, so no more of that." He looked hard at Nat.

"That's why we're here," said Nat, a tinge of irritation in his voice. And then we left, with assurances that they would be in touch with me as soon as they had any news.

Out in the daylight, with the sun shining and people going about their business, it seemed hard to believe that all this was happening to me. I was just like everyone else really, wasn't I? This would all end, and I would be able to take down the cameras and walk down the street without worrying that someone was watching me. I said all this to Nat, and although he replied with what I wanted to hear, I could tell that he didn't think it would be as easy as that. Unfortunately, he was right.

Eventually, I had an email from the detective we had spoken to last. I could have opted for a letter, or a face-to-face meeting, but I hated letters and another meeting would be stressful, especially if I had to do it on my own, so this was my choice. It was several days later, and I had been like a cat on hot bricks, checking my messages at every possible opportunity. My teaching was suffering badly, I knew it, and I was having serious discipline problems with some classes, but it was so difficult to concentrate. What would Greg say? Would his parents support the police or defend him? Children have a very highly developed system for identifying weakness in teachers, and this appeared to be working well in my case, as my relationship with classes I had hitherto enjoyed teaching now disintegrated.

That was why I was so desperate for feedback from the police. If it was good news, if Greg had held up his hands and apologised, promised it would all end, then I could start the process of repairing my life. It was not too late to get back on top. I knew I was a good teacher when I was emotionally strong, and I longed to return to those days when my heart would lift at the thought of teaching rather than sink. All the good things in my life were ebbing away, but surely the tide could be turned?

Dear Ms Barker,

My colleague, DI Vernon and I attended the home of Mr Gregory Payne yesterday evening. We interviewed both him and Mr Payne (snr) and Mrs Payne, his parents. Mr Gregory Payne denied any attempt to contact you since he was visited by the late Mr Richard McCowan and Mr Nathaniel Drury and informed us that he no longer entertains any thoughts of a relationship with you.

Mr Payne (snr) and Mrs Payne both confirmed that their son has not mentioned you for some months and has had at least two girlfriends in that period.

In the absence of any evidence linking Mr Payne to any of the communications, there will be no further action from us at present, although we did make it clear to him how seriously we would take it if his involvement was subsequently proved. However, if you continue to receive other unsolicited communications, or if you have evidence which links Mr Payne to these events, please do not hesitate to contact me, on the number below. Of course, if you would like to discuss this in more detail, please do not hesitate to do that also.

That is the gist of what it said. I don't know now, when I think about it, what other outcome there could have been, as Greg was already concealing his name and going to some lengths to ensure that his communications and presents were untraceable, so he was hardly likely to admit to anything. My only hope was that this would scare him off, and as I had received nothing in the intervening days, I allowed myself to believe in a little glimmer of light at the end of this very long tunnel.

The first inkling I had that something new had happened was when I started to get messages from teacher friends expressing sympathy for my problems. A couple of them urged me to call them, and one, Natalie, asked if I was in a union. None of them lived anywhere near me, and I hadn't contacted them for some time, so I could not work out how they knew what was happening. More worrying was the mention of union membership. What did Natalie know and how could she possibly know it? Had word about my discipline problems spread beyond the school and into other local authorities? This didn't seem likely, but there was only one way to find out so I waited until the weekend then called her.

By the end of the conversation, I felt completely sick and my head was swimming. According to Natalie, I had been posting on at least two teacher forums in the past couple of weeks, wanting advice about my current suspension. This was apparently due to the fact that I had been caught in a compromising position with a fifteen year old boy, but I had been challenging the fairness of this as he was perfectly willing and had actually made the first move. I had even made a very inappropriate joke about the situation. It did not take long to persuade Natalie that this was all completely false, and she assured me she had found it all very hard to believe, but it had seemed so real, and why would anyone make up something like that?

Why indeed? It was clear now that Greg's response to the visit from the police was not what we had hoped for. Instead of scaring him off, it had angered him, and now his campaign would be malicious rather than loving. He would wear me down one way or another, and then, when I was weak and broken, he would come and claim me. That was his plan, Nat said, but he agreed that we would delay taking this new development to the police until I felt a bit stronger. I shook violently even at the thought of explaining all this to anyone. Suppose they believed it was true? Suppose they went into school and talked to the Head? There is smoke without fire sometimes, but I did not want this kind of accusation known by anyone, regardless of how ridiculous it might seem. I just wanted it all to go away.

Nat said that Greg had obviously been scouring all the teacher forums for any with my membership, then hacked into my accounts. It wouldn't be all that difficult for someone in his line of business, and he certainly wouldn't have left a trail that anyone could follow. Now, all I could do was log in and make the necessary denials, then wait and see what happened.

I did this, with Nat at my side, and it was horrible. The anger and invective I had received from total strangers made me feel tearful and guilty, although I had done nothing wrong, and I had a real fear that some people would not accept my denials or believe that my accounts had been hacked. I wanted to delete my membership of those forums and any others that Greg might abuse, but Nat said it was important to monitor the response and counter anything else he might post. So that became another nightly task, added to checking the camera footage, filing any letters and browsing the stalking websites for stories of people in a worse situation than me. These gave me a strange sort of comfort, and I spent hours reading about women whose stalkers would approach them with threats of physical violence, including rape. At least Greg wasn't that bad.

It was towards the end of June, around the time that I would have been moving in with Olga, that the campaign started reaching out beyond the confines of my life. I was still forcing myself to go to band practice, as it was about the only form of pleasure I had left. Although I had never been able to bring myself to sing solo again, Olga and I had half a dozen songs that worked well with us singing together and the band seemed quite happy to include some of them at each gig. Sadly, my relationship with Olga had not entirely recovered from the issue with the flat, and she never asked me about Greg and what was happening. I think she found it all too difficult, as she simply could not understand how I had allowed it to affect me so badly. So, rather than cause any more discord, she carried on as if it wasn't happening, but I rarely accepted her invitations for a night out these days, and she rarely argued when I refused.

I had been looking forward to the gig – as much as I ever looked forward to anything at that time. It was at a pub well-known for promoting good quality live music, and there was always an enthusiastic crowd, so it was quite an achievement for The Butterfly Effect to have been invited to play. Practice sessions had been serious and focussed in the weeks leading up to the gig, and Anton in particular was clear that we must be as polished and professional as possible. There would be no chopping and changing the playlist and no kidding around on stage.

"If we can get a regular gig at The Stag we will be able to afford a new mixer in a few months," he said. Despite the fact that I had no idea what difference a new mixer would make, I could see that this was an important moment for the band and I resolved to do my best to make it a good one. I even practised a little at home, something I had not done for months, although it made me sad as I remembered the days when I had just started to sing, or later, when Richie would hear me and tell me how great I sounded regardless of the truth.

The gig was on a Friday, so I had little time between arriving home from school and leaving for The Stag. It was a big pub just out of town to the north, and it would only take fifteen or twenty minutes to drive there, but

Anton wanted us to set up early and I was aware that Friday evening traffic could still be a factor, so I left school as soon as I could and hurried up the front path to my flat. My heart sank as I pushed open the front door, as I could feel the weight of the post behind it, and once I was inside it was clear that there were a number of items from Greg. The packages contained a young adult novel entitled 'Young Love' and a pack of Valium tablets, or most likely something calling itself Valium but made up of cheap and dangerous ingredients. I put them to one side. Maybe they would be traceable. Maybe, just once, he would slip up, and then we would have him.

The first letter contained only a newspaper article about a teacher who had been found guilty of grooming a pupil in his school and had received a prison sentence, so that was filed, and the second was a typed sheet, filled from top to bottom with what I can only describe as a demented rant about me and my imagined behaviour. I only read it a couple of times, as it had such a bad effect on me that Nat had to take it away and keep it himself, but it was in a totally different league to anything else I had received. I was a whore and a slut. He had seen me flirting with men, unspecified men, and pupils alike. He had seen the way I looked at the boys when I was on gate duty or seeing them onto the buses, he knew what was in my mind. He knew what I got up to when I got home, about all the filthy websites I visited, and it was only a matter of time before it all caught up with me. There was a lot more, all on the same theme, and all completely unhinged.

I don't know how I forced myself to put it to one side and concentrate on getting out. Something told me that if I didn't do this, if I didn't make it to the gig, he would have won, and I still had just about enough resolve not to let that happen. I scanned the camera footage to confirm that the letter had not been hand-delivered despite the apparent stamp and postmark, and spent a few minutes - or what I thought was a few minutes - on my favourite stalking website, looking for advice about this form of abuse. That meant I had left myself much less time than I had intended, but I changed quickly, repaired my make-up and rushed out, still determined that my evening would not be spoiled.

I could see the van in the car park of The Stag as I arrived, but the sliding door was closed and there was no evidence of the others. Had they set up already? I was only about fifteen minutes late, so they must have arrived very early if that was the case. I parked and rushed inside, ready to give my apologies, but I was met by a furious-looking Anton as I entered.

"No point in going in there," he growled, "as if you didn't know!"

"What are you talking about? What's happened?" I asked, my stomach clenching, but he pushed past me and barged outside, the door slamming behind him. I didn't feel inclined to follow, so I walked further into the pub.

Olga and the others were round the corner, leaning on the bar and looking glum. They looked up as one when I approached.

"What on earth were you playing at?" asked Olga sadly. When I told her that I had no idea what she was talking about, she told me that I had emailed the landlord some weeks ago, and had explained that The Butterfly Effect had unfortunately double-booked and would have to pull out. I had signed it on behalf of Anton who, I had said, was away at a conference and could not be contacted. The landlord had not been happy, as he planned his events weeks in advance and advertised them widely, but he had managed to get a replacement and they were setting up now, as she spoke. I remembered seeing another van in the car park as I locked my car, but I had thought nothing of it at the time. It was true, the gig was off, but it wasn't me. I hadn't emailed anyone! Why would I do such a thing?

I don't know whether they believed me. I suppose they did, in a way, especially when I told them what had been happening recently, but the damage was done. I found the landlord and explained it all to him, tears running down my face, but he had no more slots for us to fill and he could hardly send the replacement band away again. Yes, he would bear us in mind if there was a cancellation. Yes, he would bear us in mind when he started his next round of bookings, but that would not be for months. Our chance had gone. They knew it and I knew it, and I could think of nothing better to do than to go home and hide, to lick my wounds and ponder on this new turn of events. I was poisonous, and now the poison was leaking out and hurting my friends and I couldn't bear it.

***

I'm tired. Physically tired, in a way that I have not been for some time. It occurs to me that I must have become incredibly unfit in recent months, as I took almost no exercise. Even when I was leaving the house, I would either drive or Nat would take me, as the risks were obviously reduced that way. Even my own street seemed like a set from a horror film, with shadows at every turn and strange rustles and sighs coming from every tidy hedge. You hear about people who are hostages, or unfairly imprisoned, and how they keep themselves fit by doing press-ups in their cells or running on the spot. How do they do that? Where do they find the strength, the energy? I felt like a prisoner, although I can't truthfully compare myself to people like that, but I could no more have done a series of press-ups than flown to the moon. It was as much as I could do to take a ready meal out of the freezer and put it in the microwave. Maybe that shows how spineless I am.

I wonder if I could sleep now, then I could carry on with forcing the screws further into the wood after I have rested, but I am hungry too, properly hungry, so I defrost some more bread and find some beans. Comfort food, and I am halfway through and actually enjoying it when suddenly I stop, the fork suspended between the plate and my mouth, as the memory hits me like a punch to the stomach. It was the day I first went back to Richie's, on the last day of term, and there was a time at some point during the evening, when he stopped kissing me and stood up as if something was wrong. It was still so soon after we'd got together that I had a worried little stab of anxiety, but he was only messing about, full of mock shame.

"How could I be so useless!" he cried. "You've been here two and a half hours and I haven't even offered you anything to eat! Stay, there, do not move, and I will put it right!"

And it was beans on toast, not unlike this, the toast over-done at one edge and limp at the other, the beans as hot as lava. It was all he could find in his cupboard, although as I found out later he was quite a good cook, and he served it on a tray covered by a tea towel. I can see him with that tray, as clearly as if he were here in the room with me. He was trying to carry it one-handed, balanced on his finger tips, but he kept nearly dropping it, and I was laughing and he was laughing and we were so happy. So, so happy. I can't eat any more and I have to stop myself thinking like this, or I will begin to wonder why I am bothering with anything, the barricade, the plans, the hopes. Even if I get out I can never be really happy, as I can never see Richie again, never hold him, never wake up and know that he is there beside me.

***

It was incredibly difficult to drag myself into school the following Monday. I barely left the house all weekend but had done very little preparation, having divided my time between a number of new websites I had found, crying on my bed and looking out of the window. If only Greg would appear. I knew it would scare me, but he might be caught on camera. There might be something to act upon, instead of this terrible limbo. Nat was away, although he felt terrible about leaving me and offered to cancel his plans, but I wouldn't let him. How many other people's lives were going to be affected by this?

So, I walked into school that Monday morning feeling like a husk. I don't suppose I looked a lot better, as I was losing weight and sleeping poorly and this had given me hollow cheeks and dark circles under my eyes. I was up in my tutor room, wondering if I had time to take down a display that had become scruffy and dog-eared, when one of the deputy heads came in. I could almost tell what was in her mind as she stood there. What on earth is going on here? What's happened to the bright young teacher who made this room a cheerful and stimulating environment for her tutor group? She may have been thinking something else, I don't know, but it didn't stop her saying what she needed to say. She may have been sad for me, but she had no choice.

They more or less took me off timetable for the remaining weeks of my contract. They actually wanted me to take sick leave, but at least I was safe in school, so I got to do a bit of cover here, a bit of small group work there and I went on a lot of end of term trips. Sometimes, when we were far away, at some educational facility or learning how to canoe, I would forget for a moment about everything. I would relax and laugh with the kids, I would feel confident to discipline them if necessary and, mostly, they would respond. Then I would go home and deal with whatever Greg had chosen to send me, or wonder what he was planning if there was nothing, and I would know that it was all coming to an end. No contract for September, no school to escape to, no income.

That's how I came to spend the anniversary of Richie's death with a group of Year 9 boys with behaviour difficulties who had earned themselves a day at a theme park. I could just as easily have stayed at home, everyone would have understood, but this was what I wanted to do. Richie had worked with these boys, talked about how he was going to use Science to re-engage them with school. He had some success with an after-school club, thinking up increasingly bizarre and exciting experiments to keep them occupied and giving them opportunities to use equipment denied to them in mainstream lessons because of the perceived risk. This was my tribute to him, much more meaningful and poignant than weeping over the plaque where his life was commemorated. I did that later of course, but I didn't want the whole day to be about what we had all lost, so I splashed down the log flume and screamed my head off on a series of increasingly terrifying rides with these boys and it was almost as if Richie was there with us.

I could hardly blame the school. If it had just been the rumours circulating about me, of course they would have dealt with it. There had already been some kind of communication to parents, assuring them that no teachers had been accused of inappropriate relationships with pupils, and that these rumours were vicious and completely unfounded. Rumours have a life of their own, and I knew they were still there on Facebook even if I hadn't been named, but it was the problem with my teaching that sealed it. They knew it was all connected, they knew I had been doing well before all this started – even after I lost Richie I was hanging on in there – but they could not let the pupils suffer. I suppose I could have challenged it, especially if they'd replaced me with another teacher on the same terms and conditions, but I hadn't the heart for it. I hadn't the heart for anything.

That's one of the reasons I didn't do the one thing I should have done, to take a holiday, but it was so difficult. The stress of it all had taken away all my energy, all my enthusiasm for life, and planning a holiday was not the only casualty of this. Now I had to think about money. With my final salary due at the end of August, I could not afford to risk any unnecessary expenditure, or I would be dealing with homelessness as well as everything else. Of course Nat said it would never come to that, and I could stay with him for a while if necessary, but I wanted to stay where I was. Once I was inside, no-one could approach the flat without me knowing it, as Nat had shown me how to get a live stream from the cameras on my laptop, and my phone was always charged and ready beside me. Greg would never get past the locks and the bolts in the time it would take the police to arrive, so at least I was physically safe, if nothing else.

So, the weeks of the summer holiday dragged on slowly, bitterly. I had virtually no contact with the band, as I had given my apologies for the last few practices. I still felt unable to face Anton even though Olga had told me that he had calmed down and accepted my version of what had happened. It was not my fault, but it was still because of me that they had lost this opportunity, and there was no escaping from that. In any case, they took an extended break in July and August, as three of them were teachers and would be away for some weeks. Facebook was becoming my only contact with the outside world, and I spent hours looking at the photos and reading about all the exciting things my friends were doing, wishing I could share these experiences but getting pangs of anxiety when I even thought about it. If I took a holiday, Greg could follow me and then I would be exposed and at risk. Maybe I was better off where I was.

It was about two weeks before the end of the holidays that Olga came round. I was watching daytime TV in my pyjamas when the bell rang and my heart started to pound. I grabbed the laptop and there she was, standing there in the sunshine, looking brown and healthy and holding flowers. My first thought was to pretend I was out. The curtains were drawn and there was no way she would know any different, but then something changed my mind. What was I thinking? This was Olga, not some stranger who could be a threat. I had seen no-one but Nat for at least a couple of weeks, as it was so much easier to get my groceries delivered and he popped in daily with anything else I might need, so it would be nice to talk to her.

I will never forget her face when I opened the door. I knew I had changed, but I hadn't realised how much until I saw her jaw literally drop and her eyes widen and fill with tears. The flowers fell to the floor as she reached out and held me in a long embrace, but we were on the doorstep and this was not safe. I scanned the street over her shoulder and pulled away as soon as I could without being rude so we could go inside.

Such a lot of tears. I really did feel as if my heart were broken all over again by the time she left, but I'd had no choice. She had come to save me, she said, to release me from my imprisonment, but at that time I saw my flat as a sanctuary not a prison and I couldn't do what she wanted. She wanted me to throw a few things into a bag and come with her, there and then. Her new flat wasn't as big as those we had looked at together, but we could manage. It was time I picked up my life by the scruff of the neck and stopped being a victim; it was time I started taking control. She had spent her holiday reading a lot of the same websites as I had, so part of me knew she was right, and it was seductive, that resurrected vision of the two of us eating toast in our pyjamas on a Saturday morning. But it was only that: a vision.

It was a vision that was far too scary to become a reality, and anyway, what about Nat? How could I throw it all back in his face, when he had devoted months of his life and goodness knows how much money into making my flat as safe as it could be? What could I say to him? "Oh, sorry Nat, but you needn't bother coming round tonight with that bottle of wine, or that box of chocolates, or whatever kind and thoughtful thing you have chosen to bring me today. No, I've moved in with Olga, yes, Olga, who I've barely seen for weeks, who said some pretty awful things about you, but never mind about that."

I don't even like to think of what she said about Nat. She said he was controlling, and she doubted his motives for helping me in this way.

"Very convenient, isn't it, having you holed up here?" she said. She was getting worked up by this time, we both were, so I don't suppose she meant to be so harsh. But the implication that Nat and I were anything more than friends really stung, especially as I had already told her I had no intention of ever replacing Richie. It was only a few weeks past the anniversary of his death, and the pain, when I felt it, was nearly as raw as the day he died. It was just that the gaps in between were longer and more manageable now, but that didn't mean I was over him. Added to that, Nat had never shown any hint of wanting me in that way. I had been Richie's girlfriend and Richie had been his best friend, so he had a duty to help me, that's all it was.

I told her all this, but it made no difference. She was beside herself with frustration and anger and goodness knows what other emotions, and she presented me with a choice: either I could do it her way, and we would live together, sing together, repair my life together, or we could do it Nat's way and I could stay cooped up in this flat like Rapunzel in her tower, waiting for my prince to rescue me. The only problem was that my prince had no intention of rescuing me, that's what she said, and I couldn't bear it. OK, so she didn't like Nat and never had, but there was no cause to paint him as the villain. Greg was the villain, had she forgotten that, I screamed. She had no right to demand that I choose between her and Nat! Why couldn't they both help me?

"I'm sorry, Amy," she said, suddenly calm. "I'm not convinced you are ready to be helped, not properly. I won't bother you again, not unless you change your mind, anyway." Then she was on her feet, sweeping up her phone and throwing it into her bag, heading for the door. If it hadn't been for the locks and bolts she would have been out before I had time to leave my chair, I had so little energy at that time, but I did manage to catch her as she finally opened the front door, swearing under her breath.

"Olga, please! Don't let it end like this, you're my best friend," I begged, but she shook her arm free and left with one parting shot.

"You only have one friend, Amy, and I think you will find out one day that he's no friend at all."

You might think that this kind of vindictiveness towards Nat would have blunted the pain of the break-up with Olga, but that was not the case. I knew she was wrong, you can't be as close to someone as I've been to Nat without getting to know what makes them tick, but I knew her motives were pure. It was what she really believed, and that was, had been, one of the things I loved about her, that complete lack of deceit. If Olga said something, you knew she really meant it, and it wasn't because she disliked Nat, or even that she was jealous of him and had decided to turn me against him. No, she really believed that he was acting out of some twisted kind of self-interest, however unlikely that seemed. So, I wasn't angry with her, not in any lasting sense, but I was bitterly sad and bereft that our relationship seemed to have run its course.

My memories of time spent with Olga were all good. They belonged in those sunlit days of sitting outside the college bar with pints of lager, walking down to catch the bus on a Friday night, dressed up and laughing at nothing much; cracking up at some funny story about school, band practice, precious moments on stage. We had so much in common we even had our own shorthand. If one of us was out, the other might text to ask about the scenery and that would elicit a response about the quality of eligible males. A question about attainment would require an answer about more intimate matters. It was silly but it encapsulated our history and Olga sometimes felt like the sister I'd never had.

That was a life I had lost, and she couldn't seem to fit into the one that replaced it, whereas Nat barely knew the old me and played such a small part in my life before Richie died that he could operate with no concern about freedoms I may have lost. All he wanted was for me to be safe, and that was all I wanted too, at the time. That's why it was no contest, but it was unbearably painful to have to make that choice.

***

I wonder what Olga would do, if she were here now instead of me? Would she be moping around, thinking about all she had lost, her head almost permanently in the past? Or would she be up on her feet, fierce and determined that he would never get the better of her? I think I know the answer to that, but I have also heard of incredibly strong women who have been worn down by a stalker, so it is simplistic to transfer the Olga I knew into this situation and imagine that she would be unaffected by what had gone before.

However, I can imagine her now, standing with her hands on her hips, rousing me to activity.

"For God's sake, girl," she says, "get off your arse and do something! Are you going to sit here quietly and submit to whatever he has in mind for you?"

No, of course I don't want to do that, but it's dark outside and I'm tired. Can't I sleep now? Surely he won't come this late in the day? But then I think maybe that's exactly what he will do. I remember with a jump that it is Christmas Eve. I remember how important today must be in his house, and I think about all the things his parents will want him to do. Or maybe he will still be at work. Lots of firms continue right up until lunchtime or even later, and then there may be social events to attend. Greg will have to behave exactly as he has on every other Christmas Eve, if he's not already in custody of course, but the evening may be his. He could still come now, and those screws are not secure, so I pull myself to my feet and get on with it. I have no choice.

It is incredibly hard. My fingers are still sore and the coin is so tiny, that each screw moves only a fraction of a turn before I have to let go, and then the coin drops and I have to find it again. The head of one of the screws is so mangled that I have to give up with that one, but the others are still worth the effort, if only my fingers hold out. Sometimes I scream with the misery of it, my voice sounding strange and detached as if there is another prisoner in here, screaming with her own pain. Sometimes I will myself into a kind of trance, push and turn, push and turn, this screw for a while, then that. At those times I get more done, or at least it feels that way, but when I finally have to stop, to let the pain subside, I see that there is still a way to go. The two screws in the door frame are almost fully inserted, but the two in the door have at least a centimetre to go and that means the slats are still wobbly, but it will have to do.

I have come to the end of my resources, so I run the cold tap and hold my hands in the freezing cold water for as long as I can bear, then wrap them in a towel and lie on the bed. Christmas Eve. I thought last year was about as bad as it could get, but it seems however bad things are, there is always the possibility they will get worse.

***

I never told Nat about what happened. Of course he knew that Olga had visited, as the camera footage showed her on the front step, showed the two of us hugging, but I didn't tell him we had parted in what seemed like such a final way. All the same, he was such an empathetic person he could tell I was unhappy, and although he didn't ask, he made an extra effort to keep my spirits up that evening, staying with me to watch a film I'm sure he never would have chosen, and keeping my mind off it all with little stories and jokes. By the end of the evening I was convinced that I had made the right choice, and the next few weeks provided further proof if ever I needed it, as that was when Greg started to get really nasty.

It was quite possibly the next day, but if not it was very soon afterwards that I started to receive the next round of unsolicited goods. I had heard of this happening to other victims, the pizza delivered late at night and so on, but this was different, as everything I received was related to my impending death. It started with a series of literature and visits from salespeople wanting to sell me life insurance. He must have put me on some sort of list, as it was unending for a while, and I had to stick a notice on the door explaining that I was the victim of a hoax and did not want to buy any form of insurance at all. So that stopped it, but then there was a whole barrage of funeral-related material, with emails about making plans for my death, links to will-writing services and a visit from the local Co-op funeral home. The poor man was very embarrassed, as the person he had been informed was dead actually opened the door, but he couldn't have felt any worse than I did.

By the end of October I had reached such a state of despair that I hardly opened the door at all, unless it was to Nat. I could guarantee that any visitor would have been sent by Greg, as there was no-one else left to visit. I had no social life, no job, next to no interaction with the outside world. In many ways I may as well have been dead, and this was a thought that occurred to me from time to time, but I never got closer than thinking about it. Sometimes, I would open the bathroom cabinet and look at the bottle of paracetamol, and I would get a feeling almost of comfort. Not today, but one day, if it all gets too much, I could do it. There would be a way out if I wanted it.

It's very strange that it was Mum and Dad who triggered some kind of a change in me. Given that they had been pretty useless parents, certainly since I reached adolescence, and any support I had received had been cold, distant and practical rather than emotional or loving, they would have been the last people I expected to come swinging into action. But that shows how wrong you can be where people are concerned.

It was just after lunch and I was debating whether I should bother getting dressed at that stage. It would only mean another set of clothes to wash and there would be nobody to see what I wore, apart from Nat and he didn't mind. But then it would give me something to do, as I had only a minuscule quantity of washing up to occupy me until the round of afternoon TV quizzes started. This was how small my life had become, but then suddenly, before I'd had the chance to make any decision, the door bell rang and my laptop screen flickered to life.

It took a few seconds to register who they were. They looked older, less upright, less sure of themselves than I remembered, but it had been a long time since I saw them away from the comfort and security of their own home. My home, it had been, but I had long since stopped thinking of it in that way. It always surprised me how many of my friends talked about 'going home' when referring to visits to their parents' homes, so I suppose I must have been the unusual one. My home had always been wherever I was living at the time, and never more so than now, when its walls were also the horizons of my life.

But what were they doing here? Although it was hardly more than a twenty minute drive from their house to my flat, I had barely seen them since Richie's death. Mum tended to phone every couple of weeks, and I would ask about their various medical conditions, she would ask about my job and that would just about exhaust our resources unless there was a cousin getting married or having a baby to tell me about, which she would do with a suitable degree of irritating wistfulness. So, when I stopped working, one half of our conversational repertoire disappeared, just like that. Our exchanges became punctuated by so many pregnant pauses – the only things likely to become pregnant – that eventually I suggested that I would call next time I had some news, an offer that she seemed to accept gratefully. By news, I meant a job of course, as she would not be interested in anything else I was likely to acquire, but I didn't tell her there was no chance of that, as I could not leave the flat in order to attend any interviews. Somehow, the fact that I was being stalked by a man whose intentions became more frightening by the day would end up being my fault, so I kept it to myself and told her jobs were hard to come by at the moment, with all the cuts to public services.

It didn't even occur to me not to let them in. Although the prospect of anything enjoyable or positive was much less likely than it had been when Olga stood in the same place, I suppose the old filial deference kicked in, as it does. You can't leave your parents standing on the doorstep and pretend not to be at home, can you? I couldn't, anyway, so I opened the door as quickly as I could and ushered them inside. To be fair to them, they made a better job of hiding their surprise at my appearance than Olga had done. However, it was clear that they did have some normal, parental feelings for me after all, as Mum was having a hard time hiding her tears and Dad was white as a sheet.

At least I didn't have to explain, as it seemed they already knew just about everything. They would not say who had told them, but the amount of detail they had led only to Nat or Olga, and my money was on Olga. Nat, having had a chequered and fragmented childhood, was less likely to see parents as a source of support, but Olga came from a large and close family. I suspected she had sought out my parents to see if they could succeed where she had failed.

And, to an extent, they did. They were not passionate as Olga had been, but they asked questions, in that way that we teachers do, and some of them were questions I found hard to answer. How long was I prepared for this to continue? What was the endgame? Why hadn't the police been kept informed as the situation had evolved?

Of course I found answers at the time, answers that were founded in the many conversations I'd had with Nat, night after night, often with a film playing in the background and a bottle of wine on the table, the film barely watched but the wine always finished. We never stopped talking about the time when all this would be over, when we would be able to present the police with the irrefutable proof that Greg was the stalker and that he was a real and physical threat to my safety. But there were no timescales as such, and this played on my mind after they left. Was I really going to live – exist – like this for the foreseeable future? Nat was wonderful in many ways, especially where technology was concerned, and if it hadn't been for him there is no telling what might have happened, but it was possible that he, too, had become trapped in a certain way of thinking. It was time to go back to the police.

So that's what we did. Nat was not at all certain it was worth it as, he said, all we had was a greater body of evidence – quantity rather than quality – and none of it led directly to Greg. But still, I had enough spirit left in me to insist, so we gathered it all up, contacted the detective I had met on the last occasion, and kept our appointment one rainy morning in November. It was November 13th, as it happened, but that did not bother me unduly. With the sort of luck I'd had in the past couple of years, I couldn't see how numerical superstition was going to make it any worse.

To begin with, the interview was positive and I was pleased we had come. Detective Wilson, who insisted we should call him Ed, was friendly and took a great deal of care when examining everything we had brought with us. He asked if we had ever seen Greg, which we hadn't, and then he tapped the end of his pen on his lips and sat back in his chair.

"Do you mind if I leave you alone for a minute?" he said. "There's something about this case I can't put my finger on, and I want to talk to a colleague."

Of course we said we didn't mind. We could hardly say otherwise, but an anxious feeling was creeping into my stomach and replacing the mild excitement I had been experiencing before. What did he mean? Was I in even more danger than we had thought? Or did he doubt our evidence?

We waited for at least twenty minutes, neither of us able to make any substantial conversational sallies. I could see that Nat was almost as anxious as me, and I felt a great rush of affection and gratitude for him as he sat there, chewing the inside of his mouth. Look what he had given up for me – goodness knows how many days of annual leave, any chance of a decent social life or new relationship – and now he was sitting in a police station worrying that the police would not believe us, after all he had done to collect every tiny piece of evidence. If this failed, he would have failed, that's what he was thinking, I was sure.

"Nat?"

"Hmm?"

"I just wanted to say thanks, you know, for everything you've done. I don't know how I would have coped without you, and even if this doesn't work, don't worry. We will get there in the end."

"Of course we will," he said, smiling and taking my hand. "I wasn't worrying, just thinking."

Shortly after, Detective Wilson – I was struggling to think of him as Ed – came back in with a woman. She was quite young, and in casual clothes: jeans, a colourful jumper and boots. He introduced her as Marie Baranski and explained she was a graduate trainee who had completed a thesis on stalking whilst at university.

"The problem is," she said, "we are not convinced that the stalker is who you think it is. We went back to see him when you contacted us again, but he was abroad, on holiday with a girlfriend. We spoke at length to his parents, who admit that he has a tendency to have what they call 'crushes' on women and to assume that they feel the same, but he is otherwise leading a normal life."

This was a massive shock to both Nat and me. Instinctively, I reached out for his hand and held it tight, and it was clammy yet cool. This was too much to comprehend, and neither of us spoke.

"Now we are not saying anything for sure, and we're certainly not doubting your evidence," said Ed, "but we have to look at this carefully. Mr Payne does fit some aspects of the profile of a stalker, and he has admitted to harassing you when your relationship ended ..."

"There never was a relationship! I chatted to him after a gig, I had one drink with him and then he tricked me into eating at his parents' house. We never even kissed!"

"OK, I was using the word loosely, sorry," said Ed, "but what I was going to say was this. You have been experiencing a continuing situation which has escalated over time. That is quite normal, if anything can be said to be normal with these people. The difficulty is that this escalation is usually matched by a deterioration and increasingly obsessive behaviour in the stalker. You would expect him to be isolated, living in his own world in which you, the object of his affections, are the centre. But here we have a man who has a functioning relationship with another woman, who is holding down his job, relating normally to his parents and showing no sign of any of the behaviours we would expect. We have to consider the possibility that your stalker is someone other than Mr Payne."

"But who could it be?" I cried, but before anyone could answer that I had to rush to the toilet. This was terrifying. At least I had known Greg. He was obviously deranged, but he was familiar. Now we were dealing with a complete unknown, someone who could be even more dangerous than we had believed Greg to be. What were the chances of being stalked twice?

Back in the room, I reached for Nat's hand again and he squeezed it.

"Are you OK to continue?" asked Marie. "We have been discussing your use of forums, and we wonder if somebody picked up where Greg left off. Did you post on any stalking websites?"

Well, yes I had. That had been in the days of my prolific use of social media and websites of all kinds. I wouldn't have thought twice about posting what had been happening to me, and I did have a vague memory of telling my story, pleased that it had a happy ending. Maybe I thought it would be encouraging to other victims – yes, my boyfriend and his mate had a word with him and it all ended. Maybe someone read that and thought 'we'll see about that'.

We left shortly afterwards. There was nothing else to say for the moment, and Nat promised he would do everything to keep me safe. In the meantime, we would go back over everything we could find to see if there were any clues. I didn't have anything else to do, after all.

"Well, what a load of rubbish!" said Nat, as we got into his car.

"What do you mean?"

"Well, honestly. All that stuff about profiles is fine, and we both know there's masses of stuff online to back it up, but I've read about cases where the person doesn't fit any of the standard profiles. Seriously, what's wrong with them? He's a bloody IT geek. He will have read all that too, and he'll know how to throw them off the scent as well as cover all his tracks. And you've met the parents! They're devoted to him. They're bound to say everything in the garden is rosy. I think he is being very clever, but I'd be astonished if it wasn't him. It has to be!"

So, I suppose that was the point at which Nat and I began to look at things differently. He could not be swayed from his opinion that Greg was the stalker, and he started to take time off work so he could follow him and photograph him near my flat, or holding a package with my address on it. A couple of times he came round all excited, saying he had seen him near enough for it to need some explanation, but the photographs were never good enough when we downloaded them. The figures in the distance could have been Greg, but they could equally have been anyone else. That, however, did not deter Nat. Even if the evidence remained elusive, he was convinced he would catch him sooner or later, and the fact that he had seen him apparently turning the corner at the top of my road was enough for him.

I did not know what to think. Was Nat seeing what he wanted to see? I remembered what it was like after Richie died – I saw him everywhere, even though I knew it was impossible. Then there would be the leap of the heart, followed by the crushing realisation. Nat wasn't suffering in that way, but his brain could be tricking him into seeing what he was looking for. Or maybe not. Maybe it really was Greg lurking around, out of reach of the cameras but close enough to see what I was doing. Was I going out? Had I started working again? He wouldn't have seen a lot at that time, but that wouldn't deter the stalkers I had read about. Nobody could accuse them of giving up easily.

In the end, I started to lean in favour of the idea of an unknown person who had read my posts and then become fixated on me. It actually seemed more likely than Greg, when I thought about it. Greg was on holiday with a girlfriend. He was working, he was getting on with his life. He was a bit odd, but was he really capable of sending all those terrible things that had blighted my life, scared me half to death, especially in the last six months? And if it was true, if it was somebody who had found out everything about me by hacking into my accounts, maybe he lived nowhere near me. Maybe he lived hundreds of miles away and was no actual threat to me at all. There had been no physical sighting of Greg or anyone else hanging around, and everything had arrived either by post or courier. It was not a comforting thought, far from it, but it was a different one and it began to affect the way I felt when I woke up in the morning.

When I say 'in the morning,' that was often not the case. What was the point of waking up when all that lay ahead of me was the tedium of daytime TV, trawling the stalking websites for any new stories or scanning the camera footage for that elusive shot that might prove Nat right and put and end to all this? That, and trying to force food into myself when I had no appetite at all was the sum total of my day, until Nat came round sometime in the evening to cheer me up.

Coincidentally – or at least I assumed it was – there was a reduction in contact with the stalker, whoever it was, about that time. It was almost as if he had exhausted every possible way of terrorising me and had run out of ideas. Maybe it was that, or the fact that Christmas was only a few weeks away, or the idea that the whole experience did not necessarily originate with a person who lived within a short drive away, but I started to become restless. I realised that I wanted to go out, to go shopping, or to sit in a coffee shop like other people. I did not want Christmas to come and go again, and to be in the same position, or worse, as I had been in this time last year. Realistically, what was likely to happen? He could hardly pounce on me in the street, and did we really need to sit and watch every minute of the camera footage? Greg had not appeared in one single frame in all the time we had been doing this, so why would he slip up now? And that was if it was Greg in the first place. These things had made me feel safe for so long, but now I felt trapped.

I said all this to Nat, one evening just before the end of November. The TV was on in the background, Coronation Street, followed by a drama and punctuated by Christmas adverts, but we were not watching it. Nat was shocked, horrified. He had obviously no idea what I had been thinking, and the panic on his features almost made me change my mind and say I hadn't meant it. Almost, but not quite.

Later, after he had gone, I felt terrible. He had begged me, pleaded with me to think very carefully about changing any of our procedures. He was absolutely certain that Greg was behind it all, and yes, he was very clever, much more clever than we could have guessed, but wasn't I still alive? Wasn't I still safe and in a position to pick up my life as soon as this was all over? Why would I risk everything now?

I don't know exactly what I said. I was crying a lot, and it all came tumbling out, all the emotion and frustration of it. I know I told him that I couldn't carry on like this much longer, and I might as well be dead if this was all my life was going to amount to. I wasn't living, I was existing, like some sort of museum exhibit, like an animal in a cage.

If I didn't start trying to rebuild my life soon I would go mad ... and then it came to me, with a punch to the head that said why has it taken you all this time? I would move. OK, some stalkers had been known to track their victims all over the country and beyond, but Greg would never leave the safety of his parents, and if it wasn't Greg, maybe if I left no trace of it online, it would be enough. I would never forget what Nat had done for me, but it was time for me to go.

My head pounded with the stress, but beneath that there was a feeling of liberation. It was the nearest I had ever got to falling out with Nat, and he left abruptly, with a sad shake of the head that said there was no point in continuing this conversation, but I was certain it would be OK once he got used to the idea. We had been through so much together, become so close, our relationship would survive almost anything. And then, when I was living somewhere else – maybe in London where it was easy to hide, or somewhere on the coast, or in Manchester or Liverpool where I knew no-one and no-one knew me – Nat could come and stay with me, and I would look after him for a change. Tomorrow, I would start making plans.

So that was how I came to be up and dressed hours before my normal time the next day, and how I came to spend a lot of time online but not on stalking websites. I didn't come to any conclusions, far from it, but every town and city I researched seemed more promising than the last. I read about dozens, in case my activity was being monitored, and I began to see myself living in their streets, shopping in their centres and teaching in their schools. I began to see myself as a normal person, living a normal life. Of course, there was a huge difference between these dreams and the reality of my life, and I didn't get further than the front door when it came to it, but there was a change. I could feel it, and it showed itself in subtle ways, like actually feeling hungry at lunch time or taking a bit more care over my hair.

I had been worrying about what would happen when Nat came round later that evening, but that was silly, of course. He is the most forgiving person I have ever known, and although he had not changed his mind, he spent only a few minutes trying to persuade me that I was wrong. Instead, he suggested that we put the issue to one side for the evening and watch a film, so we did that and we watched it properly, not intermittently, distractedly, as had been our habit. We sat on the sofa, comfortably slumped together, companionable and calm, and I found myself thinking about how much I would miss times like this, but only briefly. A bird may miss its cage for a while, but only until it has remembered how to fly.

My head was full of romantic imagery such as this in the days that followed. It's a wonder I didn't start writing poetry, there were so many metaphors for my possible freedom. However, that did not translate itself to any kind of action for over a week until, at last, I managed to leave the flat and walk to the corner shop about five minutes away. It was even more terrifying than I thought it would be. I jumped at every sound and spent almost as much time looking behind me as watching where I was going, but I did it. I don't know how long it had been since I last felt the wind on my cheeks or the rush of air as a lorry thundered past, but I bought milk and a few more items I didn't really need and hurried home again with no ill effect.

I made other sallies into the outside world in the days that followed, but still my horizons were limited. Christmas was less than a week away and I wanted to send cards, to buy Nat a spectacular gift to thank him for all he had done. I wanted to let him know that I was not rejecting his protection, but that it had run its course. Nothing was going to happen to me in a physical sense, and I had to stop worrying about all the rest of it. Some of the letters were pretty horrible at the time, so I started to burn them without reading them. I didn't tell Nat, as he would have said I was destroying evidence, but evidence had done nothing for me so far and I didn't have to read them if I didn't want to. Soon there was a little pile of fragile, wispy ashes in the grate, stirring a little when there was a draught. I'm sure I shouldn't have been burning things there, as the chimney was blocked off, but I didn't care and Nat didn't remark on it, so maybe he didn't notice or maybe he had just given up.

Nat's present was the main reason I had to push myself to go into town. I didn't want to drive, as I had no idea whether the car would start and the prospect was alarming, but I could get a bus. Nothing could happen to me walking up to the bus stop, sitting there with other passengers then walking around the shopping centre with probably hundreds of other people. That's what I told myself, and that's what I told Nat. I was not comfortable with keeping so much from him, and I had felt him drifting away from me as I became more confident. Gone were the hours spent reviewing the camera footage or poring over the letters for clues. Gone were the evenings spent discussing our next move, or some new development in monitoring equipment that he had discovered. Now he still popped in to see me, but he stayed for shorter periods and, sometimes, we found it hard to know what to say to each other. It was strange and sad, and I needed him to be on side, to help me with this new phase of the campaign, even if it had not been his idea.

I had thought he would be adamant in his opposition to the trip into town, but he did not say a lot. He had brought a bag of groceries, but when he opened the fridge to put the milk away there was a full bottle already there, and something flashed across his face.

"I see you've been out again, then."

"Yes, only to the corner shop, but it's OK, Nat, honestly. I'm very careful, and I always check the footage as soon as I get back to make sure nobody was following me."

"The camera doesn't follow you up the street, Amy. Of course he's not going to stand outside the flat waiting for you. He'll be hiding further up, you mark my words."

I really didn't think this was true, and I said so. I actually thought Nat was becoming a bit paranoid, although of course I didn't say that. But I did say that life was really a series of risks, if you think about it, and we don't weigh up the likelihood of an accident before driving somewhere, or getting knocked down by a car careering out of control before we walk down the street. There may have been risks from Greg or whoever it was, it was possible that he would be hiding in someone's front garden or would skid alongside me in a car and drag me in, but it just didn't seem likely. My street was fairly quiet, but it took a matter of a couple of minutes to walk up to the main road where any attempt at abduction would be far too risky.

Throughout this little speech, short but impassioned, Nat had been prowling around. He was looking in the kitchen cupboards, checking I had enough washing up liquid or enough tablets for the dishwasher, trying, it seemed, to find something I needed that he could provide. I felt so sorry for him, but really I had everything. At last he saw that the bin needed to be emptied and he started to tie the bag up, but I stopped him and made him sit down.

"Leave it," I said. "I'll do it in the morning. It will keep until then. Nat, you are the most wonderful friend, but you have got to stop looking after me! I owe everything to you, but I have got to start standing on my own two feet, and that includes taking out my own rubbish and catching a bus into town all on my own!"

So it was settled. I half-thought he would decide to take the day off work and go with me, which would have posed a problem as I could hardly choose his present with him beside me. Also, I was actually looking forward to doing it on my own. It would be an achievement and it would prove that there really was a future for me after all.

But I never got to do it. The idea of a future was all just a dream, a mirage, and Nat was right all along. I was so excited about the prospect of my trip, and I had spent so long getting ready, that I simply couldn't be bothered to check the footage from the camera trained on the back yard. The bin was now so full that the lid would not shut, and I felt I had to empty it before I went out, but time was getting on. It was ridiculous, the bin could have waited, but I had told Nat I would do it in the morning and it felt wrong, somehow, not to. So I took a chance. Never, not once, in the whole time we had been recording the back yard, had anyone entered it. Cats and birds were the only visitors, so what was the chance that anyone would be there on that one occasion when I didn't check?

However small that possibility may have been, it was a risk that I should never have taken. Maybe the letters I burned would have warned me. I will never know, not unless I am able to have some kind of sensible conversation with him when he comes, but I can't think about that now. The very thought makes me quiver, makes me want to be sick. Now I can only try to deal with the huge waves of regret that overwhelm me when I think of how stupid I have been. If I ever see Nat again I will apologise to him a hundred times and it will still never be enough to make up for all the time he wasted on me, only for me to throw it all away in the end. He will probably forgive me, knowing Nat, but God knows I don't deserve it.

Christmas Day

Christmas Day! It hardly seems possible that I have been here four days and nothing has happened. I can't even begin to think what it means, and I don't want to, as none of the options bears thinking about.

It looks as if it is a little brighter today, so I get the chair down from my barricade and stand by the window in case I can see the sun. When I was a little girl I was always disappointed if Christmas Day was sunny, but now I think about going for a walk before dinner, along the lane at the back of Mum and Dad's house, the sun already dipping in the sky and our cheeks stinging. I don't know where that memory came from, but it feels like a happy one, and I wonder if I have been too hard on them. Maybe it isn't their fault they make each other unhappy, or maybe they are not unhappy at all, just in the habit of appearing that way. I resolve to look at them differently if I ever get out of here, and the first thing I do will be to take them for a belated Christmas dinner.

Then I think about Nat. It's strange how I have only thought of him as my rescuer during these days, and how little I have worried about his own well-being. We had talked about spending a lot of Christmas Day together, and he had already planned the menu, saying he would cook for me. Now he will be on his own, but he will be beside himself with worry, I know that. I imagine him at the police station, demanding to speak to people of increasing seniority, demanding that more is done. I doubt he will cook anything, and he will spend the day pacing up and down, or trawling through the evidence in my flat, looking for the tiniest clues.

Of course there is the likelihood that Greg will turn up today, but I imagine he will be needed at home for the morning and the much-vaunted Christmas dinner, so I may have this morning to continue work on the barricade.

However, I have not looked at my fingers yet, and when I do, I doubt there will be any more work today as they are red raw and swollen where I have been gripping the coin between thumb and forefinger. I am useless with my left hand, so I will have to hope the screws will hold. The thought of this, the thought of him unlocking the door then pushing, pushing, perhaps shouting angrily, or whining, please Amy, Amy my love, let me in! This makes me angry, and I almost want him to appear now, to get it over with, so I can tell him what I think of him.

Suddenly, I have grown, and I am upright and fierce, shouting at the figure cowering in the doorway.

"You little shit! You have ruined my life! You have stolen my job, my future, even my ability to grieve! If you take one step towards me I swear I will kill you. I will gouge out your ridiculous fake eyes, I will tear out your blonde-tinted hair and I will rip out your heart. Bastard! How dare you talk about a relationship with me when it was obvious I didn't want it? Now, go and die; find some way to kill yourself quickly before I do it, because, if I do, it will be slow, and I will enjoy every minute of it!"

I'm shaking all over, and I realise I have said the last part of that aloud, shouting, as if he were really in the room, but I feel better for it. There is a bit of spirit left in me after all, and I wonder if I will be able to behave like that if he does get in. Maybe I really could scare him off, if I am angry enough, which I am, even angrier than I thought, so I jump out of bed and shout at the door.

"Come on then, stop hiding, you pathetic, cowardly idiot! Show yourself! Come and tell me you love me, come on, and I'll show you how much I love you!"

I hammer on the door and shout some more, but then suddenly I see myself from some detached position slightly to one side, and I'm like a demented woman, like Mr Rochester's mad wife in Jane Eyre, and I don't want to be like that. Look what he is doing to me. There is barely a trace of the old me left. Three years ago, I was at college, I was a normal student looking forward to a career; there was barely a cloud on the horizon, but all that has gone. Now, I'm either cowering within the safety of my four walls or I'm ranting at someone who can't even hear me.

This has to stop. I have to prepare. I have to assume that today will be the day, that Greg will want to share the most important day of his year in some way, but I know he will also need to maintain face with his parents. I'm certain they are not involved, so he won't be able to go out somewhere until later in the day. I think of what his mother said, that Sunday, when I thought he was nothing more than an irritation. She said she would be heartbroken, or devastated, something like that, if he wasn't there for Christmas dinner, and nobody has Christmas dinner before midday at the very earliest.

It's still quite early now, so I make some toast and a black coffee and try to be calm. I can't swallow very well and I keep gagging, but I manage to get about half a slice down and then I try to imagine what is happening in his house. Will he wake up really early with the excitement of it all? Will his mother have made up a nice little stocking for him? Will his father have donned a white beard and hobbled into his bedroom, carefully placing the stocking at the foot of the bed? It wouldn't surprise me. A chocolate Santa, a mini-aftershave, a novelty pen, a tangerine? Then they will come downstairs and she will make breakfast for them all, and there will be presents under the tree. What do you buy the stalker who has everything? I know what I would like to buy him, a hand grenade with the pin removed, but then I think of his mother's loving smile the minute before she is blown to bits alongside him and I put an end to this train of thought. It's good to be angry, but this is going too far.

Next, I try to think of how he will get out later. That might give me an idea of how long I have, and I think of him helping to clear the table and stack the dishwasher. Oh, Greg, you are such a dutiful son! Your mother will be so proud of you when she hears what you have been doing for the past two years. I start to imagine her in court, a tissue held to her eyes, and his father, frail and grey, hollowed out with the shock, the embarrassment of it, but that isn't helping either. I must concentrate, so I imagine the room tidy and clean, his parents sitting quietly in their shiny leather armchairs, perhaps with a glass of sherry. Is this the time? Is this when he can make some excuse to go out for a while? I remember the girlfriend, and I think yes, if she's still on the scene, that's what he will say. Mum, Dad, is it OK if I pop round to see Tracey, or Susan, or Arabella or whatever the poor cow is called? And he'll have a nice little present, all wrapped up in his mother's Christmas wrapping paper, but that present won't be for Tracey, or Susan or Arabella, it will be for me.

I wonder what he will have bought for me. He must be running out of ideas by now, as he has sent so many gifts already. Some of them were actually quite nice and I would have liked them under different circumstances, but this one will be different. It will be symbolic, expensive. With a shudder, I imagine opening a small package to find a little velvet box inside, and when I open that, there is an engagement ring inside. A huge diamond, or maybe something antique. I try to imagine how I would deal with that, but I can't, and my mind slips back to Richie. We had talked about marriage, and although neither of us was particularly bothered about it for the moment, we had agreed it would probably happen at some point.

"Maybe we'll get engaged when we come back from Canada," he'd said. "We could have another party. It would be a nice way of getting all our friends back together again."

I pointed out that he hadn't actually proposed to me yet, but he said I would have to wait for that.

"I've got a year or so to plan, haven't I? Don't think it's going to be here, or in some quiet little restaurant. When I propose to you, it's going to be in style, so you'd better say yes!"

I laughed and said this was a risky strategy on his part, but we both knew there was no chance I would say anything else. And now I wonder what he would have done, what spectacular occasion he would have devised. He never got the chance to plan it, or if he did, it never blossomed into any more than an idea, and I never got the chance to say yes. Sometimes I can't believe how much it still hurts, even after all this time, when I remember these odd little moments, when I allow myself to think about what might have been.

So, having worked all this out, I'm quite convinced that nothing will happen yet when it does. I hear the sound of a key being inserted, hear the lock click.

I'm sitting on the bed, propped up against the pillows, dreaming a little and wondering if I should make a drink and I am utterly unprepared. How stupid! I have been anticipating, fearing, this moment for four days and now, when the time has come, it is a surprise. I should be by the door with a cup of scalding hot water or a pile of missiles to throw at him as he enters, but there's no point thinking about that now, as I am paralysed. I shrink back, clasp my arms around my legs and focus on the door. It is partially open, but the slats are holding, and then I hear him.

"Amy! Amy! For God's sake, what have you done? Let me in."

He's speaking in a kind of stage whisper, as if there are other people around, but I know there are none, or they would have heard me any number of times before. However, although I would love to scream and yell at him, alert the whole world to my plight if only they could hear me, my voice is frozen too.

The door rattles again and I see the slats begin to shift. I can hear him still, muttering to himself and swearing as he shoulders the door, each push forcing the screws out a fraction more. Suddenly, movement returns to my limbs and I roll off the bed and wriggle my body under it. It is very tight, and I'm gasping, crying, pushing with my toes, pulling with my fingertips until I am jammed underneath. I try to get nearer to the centre but I'm stuck now, a situation that would normally fill me with fear, except there is another, greater fear to override it.

I can't actually see the door from my position, so I have to rely on my ears, and I can hear the splintering of the wood as one of the slats gives way, hear the sound of the door hitting the desk as the other one falls off. Then I can hear the desk being pushed aside, as I knew it would be, and the door closes again. I hear a click as it closes and another as the lock is turned.

"Oh, Amy, you silly girl, what have you done?" he says, and then my brain does somersaults as that wasn't Greg's voice, nor was it that of a stranger.

"Nat?" I whisper. I still can't believe it. Maybe Greg has learned to sound like him.

"Yes, it's me. Come on, out you come," he says, kneeling down beside the bed and putting out his hand.

It takes some time to get me out, as I really am stuck under there, but when I'm free I throw myself into his arms. This is the moment I have been imagining, dreaming of, all this time, and I am laughing and crying at the same time, soaking the shoulder of his jacket with tears and probably snot too, but I don't care about that and I doubt he does either.

We stay there like that for a while, probably less time than it seems, but then I open my eyes and I see the barricade all in bits, I see the fridge-freezer and the walls and the wardrobe and I have to get out, now, this minute, this second. I pull away and run to the door, forgetting that it is locked, rattling it, pulling it, kicking away the broken slats in frustration.

"Come on, unlock it, quick!" I cry. "Greg could be here any moment! We've got to get out and go to the police!"

Nat is impassive. He has not moved, but has simply turned to face me.

"You don't need to worry about Greg," he says.

"But how do you know?" I can hear my voice rising. I sound like a child.

"Don't worry how I know. It's all in hand," he says. "You have to trust me, Amy."

Of course I trust him, that goes without saying – he's here, for God's sake, he's come to rescue me just as I dreamed he would – but I can't understand the lack of urgency and I can't stop worrying. Why would he want to stay here anyway? Even if Greg isn't on his way, I still need to talk to the police, and I want to get out. I want to see daylight, I want to go home.

"Nat, please! Can we just go now anyway? I've been here four days and I'm going mad. It's Christmas Day! Let's go and tell the police, then you can cook me that dinner you promised, or we can go to a pub, a restaurant. Anything, I don't care!"

"It's not as simple as that," he says, then he comes to me and takes my hand; takes me over to the bed and sits me down, one hand holding mine, the other exerting a gentle pressure on my shoulder until my knees bend. He sits down beside me, still holding my hand, and my heart is going crazy now, but not in a good way. What on earth can he mean? What possible reason can there be to stay here? Why isn't it simple?

I haven't spoken. I think I must be going into some kind of shock, what with the fear of it all, then the relief, then this … this what? It's too much to comprehend, and I'm slumped there, head down, trying, really trying hard not to cry, because there shouldn't be anything to cry about now, it should all be laughter and relief, but something isn't right. Nat reaches up with his other hand – he hasn't let go of mine yet – and puts a finger under my chin to tilt it up and towards him. I don't resist, as this is Nat, Nat my hero, Nat my friend. Whatever is going on here, he will have his reasons I tell myself, it's just that it doesn't feel that way. It all feels wrong.

"The thing is, Amy," he says sadly, "I can't let you out right now. It's still dangerous out there, and you're a risk to yourself. I can't stand by and let something happen to you, you must understand that, so you're going to stay here. Don't worry, I'll be coming much more often. I had to go to Norwich, for work, or I would have been here ..."

"What?" I interrupt. "What are you talking about? How can it still be dangerous out there? There must be enough evidence against him now. He's abducted me, for God's sake! He's brought me here, kept me locked ..."

Oh my God. He hasn't, has he? I can tell by the look on Nat's face that Greg didn't do this, and suddenly I know that it was Nat's hand holding the cloth over my nose and mouth that morning in the back yard, that it was Nat who brought me here.

I shake myself free of him and run to the bathroom, where I vomit my small breakfast into the toilet and slump to the floor, waiting for the convulsions to subside. He's in the doorway, watching, I can sense it, and I try to clear my head. What is going on here? He must have gone mad, that's all I can think of. All the stress of the past two years has got to him, much more than I ever could have guessed, and now he is having some kind of breakdown. He is so terrified that something will happen to me, and he will have to deal with it, deal with the feelings of guilt and loss, that he has made this plan to stop that ever happening.

Suddenly, everything is fitting into place. The familiar clothes, the shower gel, the food. It wasn't Greg spying on me, it was Nat's total familiarity with every aspect of my life that enabled this room to be fitted out exactly as if I had done it myself, and it is all so clear but all so ludicrous. This is Nat, my Nat, who is calm and sensible when everything else in the world is mad. It can't be true. There must be another explanation so I turn around, kneel in the tiny space between the toilet and the door and beg him, plead with him to let me out.

"This isn't like you, Nat," I cry. "Something has happened, but we can make it alright, I promise. It doesn't matter about all this, there's no harm done. I won't go out again, I promise!"

"Ah, but that's where you are wrong, Amy," he says quietly, so quietly that it is almost a whisper. "There is a lot of harm done. You have made me stop trusting you. You don't know how many sleepless nights I've had, knowing that you are putting yourself in such danger and I doubt you would care much anyway. Do you think I enjoyed all this? Do you think I relished all the time and expense it took to get this room fitted out for you? Don't worry, I'm not expecting any gratitude. I'm way beyond that."

So at least I know I'm right. This is awful and my blood is pounding in my head so hard and fast that I think I may pass out. I want to throw myself on the bed and cry and scream, but in some little corner of my mind I feel sorry for Nat. Greg has managed to wreck two lives instead of just one, and now I have to find a way to get us both out of this.

I drink some water then he supports me back into the room. He is apparently gentle, considerate, concerned. He is just like his normal self, and he insists on helping me back onto the bed so I can lie down for a while. I really don't want to lie down. I feel vulnerable, even though it is Nat and I know he won't hurt me, but I do as he says. If I am going to talk him out of this I have to keep everything calm and avoid any kind of conflict. If he leaves without me, who knows when he may be back? If I'm right, and he is unstable, he could do anything – jump on a plane to South America, jump under a train. Then nobody would ever know what had happened to me.

It's at that point that something else occurs to me, and I have to force myself to lie still, to keep my breathing even, to allow my eyes to close as if I am falling asleep. All this time, I have been assuming that the police are out looking for me, that Mum and Dad are worrying about where I am, that the wheels are in motion. But now I realise that nobody even knows I am missing. Nat will not have told anyone, of course he won't, and it's quite possible he has used my email address to contact Mum and Dad and spin some story about me going away for a break. Oh, if only! My body is outwardly calm, but my insides are churning and my brain is spinning. How am I going to deal with this?

I lie there for a while, my eyes closed, and eventually he gets up from his place at the end of the bed and starts moving around. I take a peek when I think it is safe, and I catch a glimpse of him carrying something from the door. It looks like a cool box, the kind you take camping. What on earth is he doing with that? The next time I look he is pulling the desk back to near its original position, and getting plates and cutlery out of the cupboard. When he starts the microwave I can't lie there any longer, so I sit up and rub my eyes, hoping my actions are not too theatrical, and ask what he is doing. I hear the tremor in my voice and wonder if he hears it too.

"Dinner," he says. "I promised you Christmas dinner, so here it is. Not quite as good as freshly-served, but nothing I can do about that."

I don't reply. The implication that all this is somehow my fault, that I could be eating Christmas dinner in my own flat if only I hadn't been so reckless, is not one that I care to explore. I have to remember that Nat is not well. He would not be acting like this if he was in his normal state, and I must not make things worse, so I climb off the bed and go to wash my hands.

The little desk is set for two. There is only one chair in here, so he pulls up the cool box and puts one of the pillows on it. There are bright red napkins decorated with holly leaves and gold swirls, plastic wine glasses and even a tea light in a foil saucer. Then there are crackers, of course, and I have a vision of sitting here with a paper crown on my head, trying to be festive, and I'm not sure I can do it. However, I don't seem to have much choice, as he bids me sit down and places my microwaved Christmas dinner in front of me.

"Thanks, Nat," I say. "You really have thought of everything, but honestly, I'll be fine to go back to my flat. We can eat this now of course, it looks lovely, but I've learned my lesson. You've shown me how vulnerable I was to attack, and you can be sure I won't be going out again. Not without you, anyway," I add with the best smile I can manage.

"Not now, Amy," he says, and I can tell by his expression and his voice that this is not going to be easy. This is going to take all the patience and resolution I can muster, and I only hope I have enough.

We eat our food almost in silence. Nat is sullen, practically sulking, although I have said nothing to annoy him and certainly kept off the topic of returning to my flat, despite the fact that it is almost impossible to stop thinking about it. Eating is very difficult, especially as I still feel sick, but I force down as much as I possibly can and I'm thankful that he has obviously cooked this at home then brought it here rather than buying some dreadful supermarket offering.

"This is lovely, Nat," I say, "but it's beaten me. You know what my appetite has been like," I add, hoping this will remind him that it is me who is the victim here.

"Hmm, well I thought with all your new-found independence you might have got your appetite back too," he says, and I sense petulance in his voice. I'm sure I'm right about him. He really isn't himself, so I ramble on again about how stupid I've been, how I should have listened to him, how I should've known Greg would never give up. He relaxes a little, picks up our plates and places them on top of the fridge.

"A little dessert?" he offers, producing two small, plastic sundae glasses. "My own version of tiramisu, not very Christmassy, but I know it's your favourite."

So I have to eat that too. How can I do anything else? My whole being is geared towards detecting any changes in his mood, any opportunities to persuade him to let me go, and I can't see that rejecting his food is going to work in my favour. Normally, I would love this. It is rich and creamy, with layers of flavour and the warmth of the alcohol adding to the effect, but it is a struggle and it takes all my willpower to scrape out the last spoonful and appear to relish it. I tell him how wonderful it is, say it is the best tiramisu I have ever tasted and he seems pleased, so I have another try.

"So, shall we clear up and go now then? We can go to the flat and get back to our old routine. I'm sorry I was so stupid, but I won't be again, really."

"Look, can you stop, please? I've told you, you're going to have to stay here for the time being. I don't have any choice. It won't be forever, obviously, but I can't take any more chances and it's affecting my work, keeping an eye on you. Do you know how much time I've had to take off?"

"But you don't have to keep an eye on me! I can't thank you enough for all you've done, Nat, but I have to take responsibility for myself, don't you see? I'll be too scared to do anything now, but even if I wasn't, even if Greg did get me, it would be down to me, not you. You don't have to do this, Nat. I can see how it has affected you, but we can sort something out, can't we?"

"What do you mean, 'affected me'?" he asks. I have to back-pedal madly, talk about how much of his life I've taken up, talk about how I've expected too much of him, how much he has sacrificed. This isn't far from the truth, he has done so much for me, but I can't tell him what I really think, that the stress has tipped him over the edge, so I say I was talking about how his social life has been affected and I can't bear the thought that now his work is suffering too. I think I am pretty convincing, especially as I am wound up tighter than any spring. It's a wonder I can even string a sentence together, but it's to no avail. Nat is adamant. I have to stay here for now, whatever that means, and then it becomes clear that he is actually preparing to go, and I panic, grab hold of him, beg him.

"Please Nat, please! Don't do this! Don't lock me in here again! I'll be good, I promise. I told you, I won't set foot outside the door if you'll only let me back into the flat." I'm crying now, pulling on his arm as he gathers up the remains of the meal and puts everything into the cool box. He shakes me off, then gets his coat and takes out his phone, walking round the room, holding it out in front of him from time to time, as if trying to get a signal. I follow him, clutching hold of his sleeve like a beggar in the street.

"Stop it, Amy. You're becoming hysterical. Get a grip on yourself. You're perfectly safe here, I don't see what the problem is. No-one else is going to come. You've got food, drink, heating, lighting. I've made it as comfortable as possible and you're acting as if I'm leaving you in a dungeon. You'll be grateful one day, even if you're not now."

Somehow, I can't see that happening, but I don't want to fall out with Nat. For a start, it could be dangerous, but, also, I am still fond of him, even if he is acting completely irrationally. It's not my fault, but it's another case of the toxic side-effect I seem to have, as if I am carrying a chaos virus around with me and infecting everyone who gets too close. I never would have predicted this could happen to Nat, who always seemed so calm and strong, but there is no point in being angry with him now. It would be like being angry with my grandmother when she got cancer and could no longer care for my grandfather. Really, Grandma, this is most inconvenient! You know Granddad has dementia and needs you to look after him. You could have chosen a better time!

So I give up. There is no point in trying to persuade him, and I certainly don't want him to have to physically push me away. If he is angry when he leaves, it may be longer before he comes back, so I try to pull myself together, even though I am crying, and I thank him for the food, thank him for looking after me and ask him when he will be back.

"I don't know, Amy. I can't spend every spare minute I have round here. You've got everything you need."

And then he is gone. I hear the lock turn, and I press myself against the door so I can listen to his footsteps, but the stairs must be carpeted and although I think I can hear a door slam somewhere below, I can't be sure. It could be my imagination. He could be standing right outside this door, waiting to see if I do anything stupid, but I don't think so. I'm pretty sure I am on my own again, so I go back to the bed and sit back against the pillows as I did before.

How can I process this? When I watched the slats give way, I was terrified by the thought of Greg, or even some stranger, coming here to take possession of me, rape me, even kill me, and I don't have that to worry about now. But Nat turning out to be my kidnapper? My whole world has been turned upside down, and now I have no-one to rescue me as my hero turns out to be the villain.

But he's not a villain really, is he? Poor Nat. Now I have to think of him in a different way, as another one of Greg's victims. I have to try to look at it all from his point of view, and then I may be able to find a way to reassure him. I only hope this condition he has, whatever it is, is not too serious, or he may lose all touch with reality and then it will be hopeless. But, to my admittedly untrained eye, he did not seem psychotic whilst he was here. Moody, irritated, but still recognisably Nat. Maybe there is hope yet.

***

I've no idea what time it is now, or how long I have slept. All the emotional upheaval seems to have finished me off, and I fell asleep sitting up on the bed, no further ahead in my deliberations. Maybe there is no point anyway. Maybe I will just have to wait and see what mood he is in tomorrow.

I decide to tidy up, to ensure that everything is orderly for when he returns. I want to demonstrate that I am calm, sensible and capable. So I wash the plates and cutlery, dry them and put them away, wipe the desk down and put the napkins in the bin. That leaves only the crackers, which we didn't pull in the end, as even Nat must have realised this was a step too far.

I am about to open them up and take them apart, but then something stops me and I put them in the bin too. What was Nat doing with his phone? Why would he be looking for a signal just then? He didn't make a call, or appear to text anybody, and why not wait until he got outside and he could do it in the peace of his car? He must have driven here, as he could hardly have managed that large cool box on public transport. My guess is that he was activating a camera – I saw him do it when he installed mine outside the front door – but this will be a tiny one, hidden in a corner or concealed in the furniture. Maybe there is more than one.

I can't let him know I suspect anything, so I carry on tidying up and then I apparently kick over the bin by mistake, so the contents spill out beside the bed and I have to pick them up. As I do, I pop the crackers under the duvet and hope this won't have been noticed. If he says anything tomorrow, I will know for certain I am being watched. This is not a comfortable thought, but now I wonder if it was the same in my flat. I wonder if I have been watched for some time, and although Nat's motives may have been laudable, suddenly I feel creepy all over again.

I finish tidying, then I go into the bathroom and wash and brush my teeth. Now I have another problem. Normally, I would remove at least some of my clothes, and there are even pyjamas in the wardrobe if I want them, but the prospect of undressing with hidden cameras trained upon me makes me think again, so I turn off the light, slip out of my jeans and jump into bed still wearing my T-shirt. If Nat is watching he will have had a brief glimpse of my pants, but I don't think that is the object anyway. It is an obsessive and unhealthy interest in my safety, but I don't think he is a voyeur.

I lie still for a moment, then I move one of the crackers up the bed with my foot, slowly, until it is in within reach of my hand. Now I can work on it, and I detach the foil from the cardboard tube at one end and carefully extricate the strip. I have no idea what makes it crack when it is pulled apart, but it might be useful at some point, so I reach down and tuck it inside the elasticated edge of the mattress cover. I post the paper and cardboard under the bed, from where I can retrieve it later, but keep the gift. It is round and hard, and I bring it up close to my chest so I can look down at it. I can just about see that it is a tiny mirror in a plastic case – the sort you might keep in a handbag – and I am delighted with this. Nat must have been unaware of the quality of the gifts inside these crackers, as I repeat the exercise with the second one, and that presents me with a miniature screwdriver set. There are four of them, and they are not big enough to be any use on the furniture in this room, but I have them now and I did not have them before. That is what being here is doing to me – I look at everything and wonder how it might help me.

I tuck them under my pillow. It's pretty dark in here, so I doubt the camera will have picked anything up unless it's infra-red. I'm hoping I won't need to think like this for much longer. I'm hoping Nat will see sense and let me go, but I am a prisoner regardless of who my gaoler is, and I can't help thinking like one.

Boxing Day

It's light outside and, incredibly, I appear to have slept quite well. I suppose exhaustion takes over, eventually. I'm beginning to get a sense of time without clocks or watches and my guess is that it has been light for at least an hour, so that would make it about 9 o'clock.

I can remember the change that seemed to happen over the Christmas holidays. In December, I'd leave the flat in darkness, it would still be dark when I arrived at school and dark by the time I got home. But once the new term started, I would see the grey light appearing over the rooftops as I pulled into the car park and it would be light by the time the students started to saunter in. I lie back and wonder if I will ever have those times back again, and then I get a huge rush of anxiety as it all comes flooding back. Nat, and what he has done. Nat's mental health, which is clearly fragile and upon which everything depends. I resolve to do nothing to upset him today, to act as if I am some sort of a guest and happy to be here. That will not be easy, but I have to keep him on side.

Then I think of the cameras. I have no proof that I am correct, but today I will act as if every movement is being watched. If he is sitting at home monitoring me on his laptop, then I want him to see how sensible I am, how rounded, how unlikely to do anything dangerous or rash. I am not sure what such a person would look like, given the lack of opportunity to do anything other than stay within these four walls, but I will have to dredge up some method-acting skills from somewhere in my Drama A-level and do my best. Certainly I will have to eschew any ranting or hammering on the door today, however much I may feel like it.

On the other hand, I don't want him to know that I know, so I will have to be careful. For example, it would be very tempting to get my clothes and dress under the duvet, but that would not look normal, so I have to think this through. I could be wrong, but I suspect the cameras are confined to this room, as there would be the constant risk of them steaming up in the bathroom and he didn't go in there with his phone. That means that my only alternative is to take a shower, and the very prospect of that makes my heart thump. I have not summoned up the courage to return to that claustrophobic cubicle since the first day, and have managed with all-over washes, but I'm sure it would be a sensible idea in more ways than one. I haven't been so long without a shower since the last time I went to Glastonbury, but that was different. It was all part of the experience.

So, I appear to have resolved to chance it. Nat won't be at work, so he could arrive at any time, but I still have trouble thinking of him as a physical risk. No, the greatest risk I face is him going completely off the rails and disappearing. He has shown no sign of anything else. So I climb out of bed and choose some clean clothes from the wardrobe, taking the opportunity to hide the mirror and screwdrivers in a couple of socks as I do. Even the jeans will need changing today. My last link with my own life, my own flat, but if I am going to appear to be calm and matter of fact, wearing dirty clothes is not going to add to that impression.

I take the clothes through into the tiny bathroom and shower quickly. I know that I would not normally choose to dress in such a confined space, but I hope Nat will not think anything of it. Now I am safely back in the room, feeling better for being clean. I make some toast and coffee, sit at the desk as if it were the most normal thing in the world, and eat every last crumb. So far, so good, but now there is another problem. Apart from rinsing out my plate and mug and stowing them away in the cupboard, there is nothing left for me to do. How can I demonstrate my acceptance of this situation by sitting on the bed?

I think about what I would do if I was back at the flat. That makes me sad, but I force myself to concentrate.

Apart from trawling through stalking websites on my laptop, or following the online lives of my ex-friends, how would I fill my time? Well, for a start, there would be washing to do, and Nat will know that if he has been watching me in the flat. So I go to the wardrobe and pull the pile of dirty clothes onto the floor, where I separate it into lights and darks, just as I would at home. I don't have a washing machine, but I can talk to Nat about that later, as the basin is too small for anything other than underwear. I put the two piles back into the wardrobe and sit down again. That must have taken all of five minutes and I am going to be hard-pressed to fill much of the day in this way, but I go to the bathroom and clean the basin and shower, then I wipe every available surface in the room. I suppose about an hour has passed. Nothing looks especially different, as it was perfectly clean before, but if Nat has been watching, this can't have failed to impress.

I lie on the bed in what I hope looks like a relaxed pose, and try to rehearse a conversation with Nat. I need to tell him that I have been thinking very seriously whilst he has been away and that I have realised he is right. Of course I need to stay here for a while, so I can be completely safe. Greg does not know I am here, so none of his efforts will be rewarded and there will be the double benefit of me having a complete break from the stress of it. If I carry on like this I will almost convince myself, but really all I want to do is close my own front door behind me. The vision of that is so intense that it brings a lump to my throat.

I don't know why I suddenly remember the envelope hidden away in the wardrobe. I was thinking about something completely different, but it just popped into my head. I can't go and get it, not now, but that does not stop me exploring it and the link with this house. Am I in London? How could I tell? If only I knew the place better, but I have only ever been to Oxford Street and Covent Garden for the shops and to Leicester Square for the theatre. I think about how silly that is, when I live within such an easy distance, and I think about Nat, whose work takes him all over the country. He is so well-travelled. He even had a house here once, didn't he?

That's when it hits me. For someone who is supposed to be reasonably intelligent, I have been very slow on the uptake. Of course, this is Nat's house! The one he inherited from his aunt. I remember him telling me about his Great Aunt Ellen, and what was the name on the envelope? Mrs E Bellingham, that's what it was. I can see it, see the faded blue handwriting, old-fashioned and curly.

It's all so obvious now! How else would he be able to keep me here without anyone knowing? How else could he fit it out with all these things? He must have had some help getting the fridge-freezer up the stairs, but it would be easy enough to hire a man with a van and tell him some story about a student let. So he never sold the house after all and, it seems, there are no tenants living here either, or they would have heard me shouting and crying. That means he has been keeping it empty for some time, and I can't see why he would do that. Maybe he had trouble selling it, but that does not seem likely. A house in Camden? It would sell in no time, and that makes me worry, as it could be that he kept it empty for a reason. Did he foresee the day when he would have to take me away for my own safety, as he saw it? Is this madness of his longer term?

This is all too unsettling, so I rise and make myself a cheese sandwich. There are no more cartons of soup, and he obviously does not trust me to have tins, with their sharp-edged lids, so I force myself to sit there and eat it as if it is a nice little deli sandwich I have popped out to buy. It's amazing the pleasure you can get from a fantasy and this miserable offering has also generated a little more washing up, a few crumbs to wipe away, a few more aimless minutes used up in this pretence that my life has become.

It is actually a relief when I hear the lock turn, although I nearly jump out of my skin and hope Nat doesn't spend too long reviewing this footage when he gets home. That was hardly the action of the chilled-out friend and visitor I am trying to portray. However, I manage to calm myself by the time the door opens, and there he is. Casual but smart, looking exactly like my old Nat, the one I could rely on, the one who was the most sane and sensible person I knew. Could this all be a mistake? Have I somehow got it wrong? But I don't think so, as he has already locked the door and put the key away in his pocket, and that is not the action of a man in full possession of his senses. Not when it's his friend he is locking in, and she wants to go home.

I switch on my smile. I must not show any of the tension I feel, so I talk at the same time, but I'm rushing it, I can tell. There is no cool box today, instead he is carrying a sports bag, and he looks around for somewhere to put it, deciding on the space between the wardrobe and the door. He sees my eyes looking at it but he says nothing, takes off his coat and lays it on the bed, at the bottom. By that time, my speech has dried up. Whatever I was saying, he wasn't listening properly anyway, and I am conscious of appearing like a puppy desperate for some attention from its owner when he or she returns to the house. If I had a tail, it would be tucked between my legs but twitching hopefully and this is not how I want to appear. So I stop hovering around him and go to sit on the bed.

"Did you sleep well?" he asks. I don't have to lie on this occasion and I tell him I did.

"I've also had quite a long time to think," I add, hoping that he will say something about all the domestic duties I've been engaged in, and thus confirm my fears about hidden cameras. But he sits on the single chair and says nothing, merely arching one eyebrow, so I continue.

"Yes, I've been thinking a lot about what you said, and I know I must have appeared a bit negative, but now I see you are right. If I stay here, not only will I be safe and Greg will be isolated, but I will also have a complete break from the stress of it. It will be like a holiday. I was thinking about planning one, but this is even better, as I don't have to worry about whether he will follow me."

"Exactly," he says, in that voice that says 'why did it take you so long'. My antennae are up, feeling the air, sensing the atmosphere. Is it working? Does he believe me?

Of course it is far too early to say. It will take a lot longer before he will completely trust me again, and then goodness knows how long to persuade him, one tiny step at a time. I have to work hard not to be discouraged, as in my waking dreams he was practically ready to release me there and then, but I imagine I am on a frozen pond, trying to get to the other side. The ice is very thin in places, so I have to choose each step with care and sometimes I have to stop, go back, or slither forward on my stomach, testing out the ice with my hands in front of me. That is how careful I need to be.

There is a space between us. Not much of a physical space – that's only a matter of a metre or so – but a yawning great chasm in our conversation. We used to chat away for hours, but then I remember that the subject was either Greg or how we could defeat him. Now, with me here, we don't need to talk about that with such urgency. However, we can't sit here like this, like two people who met once at some function and have been thrown together by circumstance, neither with any desire to talk to the other. There is a danger that he will give up and go, and then I don't know how long it might be before he comes back. I can't persuade him that I have changed if he's not here, so I ask him about the house.

He doesn't seem to mind that I have guessed whose house it was and remembered roughly where it is. Of course I don't tell him about the envelope, but I appear to have developed a sudden and intense interest in property development and try to engage him in telling me his plans. Then I remember the sad and awkward conversation we had when I first heard about the house, when he was talking about buying locally, and I have an idea. It is not a very nice idea, as it involves playing upon his loneliness and his desire to look after me, but in the circumstances, that is the least of my worries.

"Have you ever thought of converting this place into flats?" I ask.

He tells me it is already converted into a ground floor and first floor flat and that both are empty, so I make my eyes grow wide and try to sound excited.

"Really? That's interesting. It's just that I had an idea – tell me if it's crazy – but I was thinking, why don't I move here permanently? We could do up the flats – if they need it, of course – and live in one each, like you suggested before."

I stop, trying to read his face for a clue to his reaction, but Nat can hide his feelings very well, and he isn't giving anything away, so I feel I have no choice but to continue.

"How big are they?" I ask. "Maybe you could show me around sometime, not now of course, but are they two-bedroom flats? What do you think?"

"I wouldn't rule it out, renovating them that is," he says. "I have always intended to sell them, as I told you, but I never got round to it, what with all the time I've spent round at yours."

"Oh, Nat, I'm so sorry! I know it's been such a tie for you, and I must seem like such an idiot, throwing it all away for no reason, but I am serious about it now. I am going to listen to everything you say. Will you think about my idea?"

He says he will. Not with a great deal of enthusiasm, but I do sense a slight thaw in the atmosphere, so I make us both a drink and we sit there in a slightly less difficult silence until I have another idea. I need to make the option of returning to my flat seem more appealing than sitting here, so I ask if he has watched any good films recently, ask about the Christmas TV programmes, talk about films we have watched together. I am trying to conjure up the picture of the two of us snuggled up together on my sofa – not cuddling, we never did that – but both in the same space. It actually makes me sad to remember it, as I know it can never be like that again, even when he is better. How can I ever feel the same about a man who waited for me in my own back yard, who held a cloth impregnated with what I assume must have been chloroform over my nose and mouth, then further sedated me so that I slept long enough to be transported here? No, those days are gone, regardless of what happens with Greg, but he must not know that.

It's later now, and we are getting on quite well. He had some jacket potatoes in his bag, and a selection of meats and cheeses, so we microwaved the potatoes and spread everything out on the desk like some sort of buffet. Then we sat together on the bed and ate, and he started to relax, I could tell, and told me about something that had happened at work. It wasn't that amusing to be fair, but I laughed and told him how funny he was. I even put a hand on his arm, briefly. I am playing my part, and it's working.

I decide to go back to the idea of the conversion. Surely there is nothing more designed to show my commitment to him than the idea of living under the same roof, so I ask if he has any paper and a pen, but he has better than that. He has a tablet in his bag, and it has a drawing app that enables him to show me how the two flats are laid out. The room I'm in is not part of either of those, but is an attic room on the second floor.

"This could be a shared space," I say, sounding excited. "We could make it comfortable, put a nice big screen in here, a big, squashy sofa ..."

I have to stop at that point, as this is all reminding me of Olga, and the days when we were planning our flat. Oh, if only I had gone ahead! If only I had moved in with her, I have a feeling that it all would have stopped. I don't know why, but I can't imagine Greg transferring all his energies to a different address. That is silly, of course, as stalkers routinely track their victims across much greater distances than the couple of miles we were thinking of, but I can't help believing that was one of the most important mistakes I have ever made.

Still, we are getting somewhere, as now Nat is talking about the flats. He is wondering whether it would be better for me to have the one on the first floor, and I say I'd be happy with that. He thinks it would be better for me to use his address rather than have one of my own, and then we talk about my new name. Of course I will need a new name if I am going to disappear from Greg's life, and we try some out. I would prefer to remain as Amy and to change only my surname, but he thinks we need to be more radical, and now he is deciding on the name, making it clear that he is the guiding force in this process. I'm not going to argue with that. It's exactly what I want him to believe.

"I think Alice Wilson will do nicely," he says, getting his tablet and typing it out so I can see how it looks. I agree to it, and it is quite difficult to keep a degree of detachment as the plans become more developed. I am throwing myself into this role, and I know he is convinced as I have not seen him this animated for some time. I almost see myself in one of these flats, choosing the paint, choosing the carpets.

But that is when it all starts to go wrong. I make the mistake of talking about teaching, about getting a job in London once we are settled in. I say I want to be able to pay my rent, but he looks at me sadly, as if I am a child he has just spent a whole lesson trying to help and none of it has worked.

"But Amy, you won't be going out. Don't you see, that's the whole point of it? Elimination of risk. We can't do that if you are travelling around London!"

Now I really blow it. What an idiot! I could easily say 'oh, of course, silly me,' and possibly get the conversation back on track, but I don't. I'm too shocked by what he has said to go along with it, and the differentiation between the fake Amy who would agree to live with him and the real Amy who is acting a part becomes blurred. I start to ask him why it would be risky if I'm living in London under a different name. Surely the trail would be too cold for Greg to pick it up here? Even if he knew I was in London, how would he ever find me? But Nat is having none of it.

"You haven't got a clue, have you?" he says, getting up. "I thought this could be the answer, but you are clearly no closer to understanding this situation than you were before. I'm very disappointed in you, Amy."

He could hardly be more disappointed than I am with myself. All that work, all those hours carefully building up that picture, me and him in two nice flats, coming up here to watch a film together, and it's all destroyed. He gets up to leave immediately, and refuses to say when he will be back. He ignores my apologies, my pleas, and with nothing more than a quick look around the room to make sure he has left nothing important behind, he is at the door.

"I have your Christmas present in this bag, Amy," he says, waving the sports bag at me. "You didn't deserve it yesterday, but today I thought you had really changed and I was looking forward to giving it to you. You've spoilt it all, and now I will have to take it home again."

He's gone, and I throw myself onto the bed and cry. Now what can I do? I am probably further away from persuading him than I was yesterday, and I am also seriously worried about his thought processes. This is way beyond some kind of minor stress-related over-reaction. He really wants me to stay inside and never go out again, and that is a serious obsession with no hold on reality. It makes Greg's actions pale into insignificance. What on earth am I dealing with here, and how am I ever going to get out?

December 27th

Oh, how different I feel this morning. Yesterday I had my strategy to work on and I'd had a reasonable night's sleep, but today all my plans are in tatters and I have spent the night tossing and turning, dreaming of all sorts of secret routes out of here. In one dream, the house had expanded to some kind of labyrinth, with so many doors and corridors, hatches and tunnels. I had Nat's tablet, and all I had to do was find the folder where the plans were saved and I would be able to follow the route, but I kept losing the tablet and finding it again, kept turning a corner to find I was in my own flat again only to realise it wasn't really my flat at all, kept taking the wrong path and having to squeeze through dark, narrow spaces.

I feel as if I've been beaten up. My head is aching and heavy and my eyes are sore, but all that is nothing compared to the sickness. I don't have a bug, the food was perfectly fine. No, I am sick with worry. It doesn't seem possible, but I am beginning to think it is a long time since Nat had any intention of supporting me back into the outside world, and I'm afraid he is much more ill than I could ever have guessed.

Still, I have to do something. The alternative is to sit around and let events take their course, but I can't do that. It seems I still have some reserves left, so I try to think of something that will either give me some control or provide me with information. Information is power, there is no doubt about that, so I turn my attention to the issue of the cameras. If I can establish their existence, without letting Nat know, that must lead to some kind of advantage. Maybe I can enact some little scenario that will provoke him into doing something I want. I don't know, it may be pointless, but I think I know what I'm going to do.

I get up and sit on the edge of the bed. I really do have a headache, but I exaggerate its effect and massage my temples before standing up. Next, I get a cup and walk slowly into the bathroom, wobble a little as I fill it with water, steadying myself on the basin. There could be a camera in here after all and I don't want to waste any opportunities. Then I walk slowly towards the desk, but before I get there, I stagger again before falling to the ground and spilling the cup of water.

I lie there for a minute or two, possibly less, then I pull myself up on my hands and knees and crawl over to the bed, where I apparently manage to stand up long enough to almost fall onto it. I wriggle up until my head is on the pillows, then I close my eyes. I will lie very still so he will wonder whether I am unconscious, and then later, maybe he will be sufficiently concerned to take me to a walk-in centre where I will tell anyone who will listen what has been happening. Of course I know that won't happen, he won't take me anywhere, but it is a nice idea, and I allow myself to let it run, to imagine all the fuss the nurses would make when it all came tumbling out. Then they would need to check me over, but I could be back in the flat by this evening.

***

So, it seems my pleasant little daydream turned into a proper sleep and I feel better. My head is still a little muzzy but, although I am still anxious and tense, the worst of the sickness seems to have dissipated too and I think I will be able to function. However, I remember that I am still performing; everything I do from now on will have to be planned and considered. So I make a show of rising slowly and sitting up for a while, rubbing my temples. Next, I wash and dress – I can't stand the thought of that shower cubicle – and eat a slice of toast. The bread is running out, and I think I must remember to ask Nat for some more. That would imply I am resigned to staying here for a while.

Now it must be about the time Nat arrived yesterday, so I start to prepare for him. I do everything slowly, sitting down frequently to rest, and I run my hand over my forehead at intervals. If I ever get out of here, I might take up amateur dramatics instead of singing, I think bitterly. I push aside the nasty, insidious thought that there is actually only a small chance that I will ever be able to make that choice. If only I hadn't lost so many friends. If only I had a better relationship with my parents. It could be weeks before they begin to doubt whatever Nat has told them, or I wouldn't be surprised if he is using my laptop to email them purportedly from some far away retreat where I am escaping the stress of the past two years. I could be dead by the time anyone begins to look.

But still he doesn't come. I am running out of things to do, and I can't spend the whole day walking around looking shaky. I'm beginning to feel like the heroine in a silent movie, all dark eyeliner and silk, wafting around with a tragic look on my face. I have to be careful not to overdo this, so I make myself another slice of toast and a cup of tea, eat it as normally as I can, then wash up and clear away with more bounce in my step. There, the Amy on film is feeling better. She had a bit of a funny turn, but now she is back to her old self and she is very sensible. Look how sensible she is, Nat! Look how she has taken the almost-empty bread wrapper from the freezer to remind her to ask for more. Look how she is putting the dirty clothes in two neat piles in front of the wardrobe, so she will remember to talk about laundry.

That kept me occupied for a while, and I have allowed myself another little rest on the bed, but now it is getting dark outside and I am still alone. Have I driven him away? Has he washed his hands of me completely? That doesn't seem likely, and anyway, he could hardly sell the house with me locked in the attic bedroom, alive or dead. But there is the risk that he has done something stupid or lost the plot completely. Suppose he was so angry when he left, that he drove like a madman and crashed the car? He could be dead, or in a coma in hospital and no-one would ever find out about me. Or suppose he went completely mad and had to be locked up? They would think I was a figment of his fevered imagination.

I don't want to cry on camera, that is going to spoil the impression I'm trying to give, so I take a cup to the bathroom and drink some water, composing myself as I do. The Amy that looks back at me is pale and haggard, so I won't have any trouble acting that part. But I must not look tearful, so I splash my face with water and dab it dry. I will do, but I don't know how long I can keep this up.

I'm back on the bed again, almost resigned to dying a slow death here in this room, when the lock clicks and I'm on my feet. I have to resist the urge to run to the door and hug him, my gaoler, the man I thought was my friend, as that will imply that I am not happy here in the peace and tranquillity of the haven he has made for me. Instead, I smile a friendly smile and ask if he would like a drink. I busy myself fetching the water, heating it, making up the dried milk and all the time trying to work out if he has been watching me.

It doesn't take long to confirm that I was right. Not only does he remark on my pallor and ask after my health, but I also catch him bending to feel the damp patch on the carpet where I spilled the water. It is visible, but I doubt he would have noticed it in normal circumstances.

"What happened here?" he asks.

"Oh, I'm sorry about that, but it's only water. I dropped a cup this morning."

He doesn't reply, but he looks different today, softer, more concerned.

"Are you sure you're OK?" he says later, as I reach across to take his cup. "No, let me do that. You stay there. I don't think you can be eating enough. I'm going to make us some food and you are going to rest."

So, now I know. He has been recording me and he has been watching the footage. I don't know whether he sits and observes my every move in real time, or whether he scans it later as we used to do at the flat, but at least I have that knowledge, that information. It means I can be careful not to give anything away, and it means I can plan and act out what I want him to see. I feel a small bud of excitement in my stomach, alongside the anxiety. I'm not giving up yet.

Meanwhile, Nat is busying himself with the contents of his sports bag. I offer to help but he waves me away, insists I remain on the bed. He has various foil-wrapped packages which he brings to the desk and arranges in a line, then he sets about unwrapping them and putting the contents onto plastic plates. He is whistling a little tune as he works, and this is very heartening, as I did not know how to respond to the sullen and argumentative man who was here yesterday and this one is more like the Nat I know. Maybe he was just having a bad day, or maybe he needs me to be weak and vulnerable in order to be happy. Well, that's a part I'm happy to play for as long as it takes, so I sit there looking vaguely pathetic and watch him getting everything ready with what I hope are big, grateful eyes.

After a while, when everything appears to be ready and the microwave is whirring, he goes back to his sports bag and takes out a present. I can tell it is a present, as it is wrapped in red and gold Christmas paper and decorated with a golden ribbon, split and pulled into a multitude of spirals. Somebody has taken a lot of care with this, but I cannot help feeling sad. Who wants to receive a gift in these circumstances? Still, receive it I must, so I fake an excited smile as he walks towards me, holding it out.

"This is what I have been wanting to give you since Christmas Day," he says. A little cloud of disapproval of my previously unreasonable behaviour dulls his smile for a moment. "But that's all behind us now, isn't it? I hope you like it."

Actually, it is beautiful, and I do like it. Even here, even in this most bizarre scenario, I cannot help but recognise the quality of this gift. It is a pure silk dressing gown or robe, in the softest, palest dove grey that looks silver as the light hits it in one way and then blue, and then silver again. I hold it up, feel how the fabric hangs in ripples and waves, as if someone had fashioned it from a twinkling stream on a summer's day. Every seam is overstitched in silver, and I don't have to act at all as I hold its softness to my face.

"Oh, Nat, it's wonderful! Fantastic! Thank you so much! It must have cost a fortune, and I love it."

He tells me to try it on – over my clothes of course – so I do, and it fits perfectly. I suppose there's no surprise there, given his intimate knowledge of my wardrobe, but I do not dwell on that thought. Maybe I was panicking too soon as I imagined all those dreadful endings. He must be very fond of me to spend so much and to choose so well. Surely there is something to build on here.

I decide to wear the robe whilst we eat. I can't bear to take it off, I tell him, and he smiles.

"I want you to be comfortable," he says and I don't say a word about how much more comfortable I would be in my own flat – I have learned my lesson in that respect. So I tell him how well he has anticipated all my needs, ask for another loaf, and even raise the issue of my laundry with nothing but a positive response.

The meal is very good, despite having been transported from wherever he prepared it. We start with olives, sundried tomatoes and ciabatta bread with oil and balsamic vinegar, and then there is his home-made lasagne, which he knows I love. It occurs to me that it would benefit from the addition of a little salad, and there is a lettuce in the fridge, so I get up and open the fridge door to see if it is fresh enough to eat.

"What are you doing?" asks Nat.

"I'm just having a look at this lettuce," I say, taking it out of the crisper, "but actually I think it's had it. Never mind."

I sit down again, but then my heart begins to thump and the blood sings in my ears as there is a very different look on Nat's face.

"You are unbelievable," he says, and I know better than to ask why. "I have never known anyone as unappreciative as you. I go to all this trouble, spend the whole morning making this lasagne for you, knowing it's your favourite, and this is how you repay me! Lettuce! Fucking lettuce! You wouldn't see an Italian fussing about lettuce if somebody served this up for them. It's just typical of you, Amy, nothing is ever good enough for you. Whatever I do, however much time I spend choosing things, you always throw it back in my face."

There is more, much more. He is raving, there is no other word for it, and it is as if he has had all this stored up inside him for months, years even, and the mention of lettuce has broken the dam. I can't imagine what I've done to deserve it, and I can only assume it is part of his illness, but I am genuinely scared as I sit there and look at his face, red with rage, eyes narrowed, spit flying from his mouth. He is a man possessed and I can only sit and wait for this to end, as I am afraid of what might happen if I attempt to move.

Eventually, he calms down, but only after he has swept the lasagne into a carrier bag. I find myself thinking what a waste that is, but really I am more worried about how this will end, as now he has turned his attention to the gown.

"You'd better give that back to me too," he growls, grabbing hold of one sleeve. But I beg him, tell him how much I love it, tell him how sorry I am about the food.

"It wasn't a criticism, honestly," I say. "I know it was thoughtless, but ..."

"There is always a 'but,' isn't there, Amy?" he replies, and then it is just like yesterday. He is gathering everything up, preparing to go, but this time I don't try to stop him. Although the thought of being left here is terrifying, the thought of being with him in this mood is equally bad, so I retreat to the bed and wrap the gown around me, hoping he will change his mind about taking it. It has symbolic value, and if he takes it home it will prey on his mind, allowing him to feel angrier and angrier, whereas if I wear it here, wear it continuously, he will see me enjoying it and maybe mellow a little. It is a forlorn hope, but the only one I have right now.

I'm on my own again. The room is a mess, with the ruins of the meal spread over the desk and wrapping paper and ribbons on the floor. He has taken the uneaten lasagne away with him, but there are balls of crumpled foil on the microwave and a little plastic bowl of oil has been spilled and is trickling down the side of it. Part of me is thinking about what I could glean here. What use might there be for foil? Is it worth keeping the wrapping paper? But everything I do will be recorded, so what is the point? Gone are the days of barricade building, of inventing ways to escape. My only hope now is psychological manipulation, and I appear to be spectacularly bad where that is concerned. I decide that a few tears might be understandable, and I'm not sure I can stem them anyway, so I throw myself on the bed and sob.

I'm spent. This is how I felt on the first day, when I'd been hammering on the door and screaming for an hour, but things are so much more desperate now. Can I stop shaking and focus again? Is it worthwhile anyway? I decide to get up and tidy away the debris in the hope that it will help to clear my head, but just as I'm on my feet, the lights go out.

It's very dark, as only a weak glow comes in through the small, frosted window at the best of times, and I've had at least one light on since the day I woke up and found myself here. Even at night I have slept with the microwave door open, as it gives me enough security to allow sleep, but it's closed now. I slip off the bed and feel my way over to the desk then across to where it stands, on the little bedside cabinet. I open the door, but nothing happens and I realise that it isn't just the lights, it is the sockets too.

This is my punishment. This is what you get for having the audacity to fancy a bit of lettuce with your lasagne. Of course there might be a power cut, but I don't think so. I think he has everything controlled by his phone, and he is sitting at home now feeling some kind of righteous justification at leaving me in the dark. Presumably the heating will go off soon too, but I don't suppose he will care about that.

I get back into bed. Strangely, although I would never have believed this, I find the dark is quite comforting. For a start, he can't see me, so that is a bonus and I know this room so intimately now that I am certain there is nothing to fear within these walls. There isn't even a spider hiding in a corner that I don't know about. That, and the knowledge that nobody, apart from Nat, even knows I am here, means that I am quite safe until morning at least. So I take off the silk gown and wriggle under the covers fully dressed, thinking that a good night's sleep will do me no harm.

Unfortunately, sleep does not come, even though I lie still and try to empty my head. Something is troubling me, a worrying, nebulous little thought that dances around the periphery of my consciousness like a sprite, teasing me with its proximity, with its transparency. It's something Nat said, a word or a phrase, something that jolted me at the time but then got pushed to one side by his anger, by the crackling tension and the fear. What was it? If only I could see the camera footage like he can, but I doubt he would find that section very easy viewing. No-one likes to see themselves out of control.

I try to imagine I am watching us. I pretend I have a laptop, and I can see us sitting at the desk, in the slightly blurred monochrome that became such a familiar part of my life. What happened? I am sitting on the chair and he has pulled the desk close so he can sit on the bed. I see myself rising and going to the fridge. I find the lettuce, the lettuce looks limp, so I sit back down. He stares at me, his eyes cold and hard, and asks me what I was doing so I tell him and his face darkens and he says ... he says I am ungrateful. No, that's not right. That's it! That's what I've been trying to remember! He didn't say ungrateful, he said I was unappreciative, and I thought at the time, briefly, that's an odd word to use. But now I'm getting a shivery feeling creeping over me as I know where I've heard that word before, and it wasn't Nat who used it. It was Greg.

It was in the first nasty letter. I read that so many times I could practically recite it, and I know I am right. But I don't think Nat read it more than once or twice, so I can't see how he could have accidentally picked up on the language. In fact, now I think of it, Nat's rant this evening was very like some of Greg's later letters and that is even more worrying. What does it all mean? What did Nat mean about choosing things for me? My mind is spinning and I can't make sense of anything. Nat and Greg seem to be getting muddled up in my head, so maybe it is me going mad after all, but then another memory hits me and my blood runs cold.

When you read that in a book, you think it is a metaphor. It's not even a very original metaphor, and I wouldn't be surprised to find it in a Year 8 creative writing exercise on building tension. But what you don't realise, until you have been very, very scared, is that it is much more than a metaphor. I actually feel as if there is ice-water in the veins of my arms and legs, and all the little hairs are standing up on end, because I can remember Greg's letter, and I can remember the silk scarf he complained I never wore. It was a lovely scarf, in a deep bronze hue, and the edges were beautifully finished with gold over-stitching and I know – in the way that sometimes you know things, without any evidence but without any doubt – that my new robe and that scarf were made by the same people. Oh my God.

Now that I have thought it, it can't be unthought. Until a few moments ago I was dealing with a stalker who was certainly scary but tended to keep his distance, and a dear friend who had become a little unstable due to the stress of supporting me through that. Now I appear to be dealing with a friend who is way beyond unstable, and seems to have invented the stalker. Can this really be true? Surely he can't have sent all those things, written all those letters?

The more I think about it, the more likely it seems, and it resolves all the unanswered questions. Why were Greg's parents and the police so sure it wasn't Greg? Because it wasn't. How did Greg appear to be leading a perfectly normal life despite being apparently obsessed by me? Because he wasn't obsessed at all – at least, not after he was warned off. Why was Nat so keen on using technology to protect me? So he could watch my every move without even coming to the flat.

If all that is true, and I'm certain it is, Nat must be suffering from a serious psychological disorder. I wonder if there is a name for it, this obsessive need to keep me safe? Then I think about Richie and the way he died, and I'm sure that was the trigger. The person he was closest to died in the most shocking circumstances and, having lost other people in his life, he resolved to stop anything bad happening to me. Obviously there is then a big jump from that thought to inventing a risk, but I can see how it happened. If he was going to be able to relax, he had to know I was safe. To know I was safe he could either live with me – and I rejected that – or he could watch me. Hence the cameras. To him, in this heightened state of anxiety about my safety, it would not be strange to pretend that Greg was still a risk. The world was risky and I needed to be protected from it; the end would justify the means.

So now I understand. Everything that has happened to me, from the moment of Richie's death, is crystal clear and there is some relief in that. At least I know what I am dealing with. However, the situation is even more serious and complicated than I thought, and I have no psychological background to help me, apart from a bit of child development which is unlikely to be helpful.

What should I do? If I do nothing, merely submit to what he has planned for me, I will be here for the rest of my life, as this meets all his needs but none of mine. But if I do something and it turns out to be wrong, who knows what it might provoke? Is he capable of violence? His behaviour yesterday leads me to think he might be, but then there is the concern, the tenderness. I have to believe that the need to protect me will overcome everything else. If I don't hang on to that, I may as well give up.

It's still dark. I suspect he will leave me without power all night, to demonstrate his disapproval and exert his control, but I can use this darkness. I need to get my treasures and hide them in a safer place, somewhere I can retrieve them without his knowledge, and the only place I can think of is the bathroom. Slowly, quietly, I inch towards the edge of the bed, still breathing deeply as if in sleep. It seems crazy to imagine that he has super-sensitive microphones installed, but nothing is impossible. Now I am lying as close to the edge of the bed as I can get without falling out, so I slip one leg out and let it fall, wriggle a little more, and then the other, so I am beside the bed, on all fours.

I wait a while, then move across the carpet to the wardrobe, keeping as low to the ground as I can. This is the easy part, but now I have to open the door, pull the drawer, find the two socks containing the mirror and the screwdrivers, all in the pitch dark and without making any noise.

Somehow, I do it. Every tiny sound is like an explosion in my ears; the creak of the door, the slight clunk of the drawer as it slides open. But I have my treasures in my hand, and now I creep back across the carpet, forcing myself to be slow, and back into bed. All I have to do now is to act waking up, feeling my way across to the bathroom and going to the toilet, making as much noise as I like. So I do all that and ease the lid of the cistern up with one hand as I flush with the other, posting the mirror and the screwdrivers in. The sound of the water flushing hides any sound they make as they drop, so I can wash my hands and return to my bed. Job done. I don't know how, or even if they will be useful to me, but they are all I have and now they are safe and accessible. I wish I could say the same about myself.

December 28th

Something wakes me early. I don't know how early, but it is dark outside, and then I realise that it is the light from the microwave. I suppose I could be wrong about Nat, it could have been a very long power cut, but I don't think so. I think he couldn't resist having a look at his little caged creature, and he needed light to do that so he switched the power back on. I slip out of bed and pad across to the main light switch, and yes, that is working too, although I switch it straight off again and return to bed. I don't want to make his life any easier by flooding everything with light and I even close the microwave on the way, as if I had left it open by mistake. In any case, it is freezing in this room this morning and I need to wait until the heating kicks in.

Now I curl up and pretend to sleep – that will make interesting viewing for him – but in reality there is no chance of that. My mind is buzzing with all of yesterday's revelations, if they can be described as such. I go through it all once more, minutely. Have I got this wrong? Is Nat really responsible for all the misery I have endured? But, unfortunately, it all seems clearer than ever today and I cannot escape the fact that I have been Nat's victim for the past two years and Greg is merely the more or less harmless eccentric I first thought him to be, all that time ago. The only positive I can find is that Nat needs me. OK, he needs me in a completely unhealthy and obsessive way, but I would imagine that he needs me alive, and to continue living is about all I can hope for, at least for the moment.

So now I have to decide what to do. It really is crunch time. I remember Dad asking about the endgame and I didn't really have an answer – only that we would go back to the police when we had gathered enough evidence – but I am at that point now. This is the endgame. It occurs to me that even if I try to spin it out for days or weeks, we can't continue as we are. Something will happen. I will say something he doesn't like and he will snap, and then who knows? He thinks this is what he has wanted all this time, but already he is finding it hard to manage. I have to find a way to make the past seem more attractive than the present. Persuade him that we can go back to that if only he will agree, but how?

I'm drifting in and out of sleep now, and Richie keeps coming into my mind. I wonder what he would do in this situation, and then I think that he may actually be the key. If I can help Nat to remember how things were before Richie died, how light-hearted we were, what fun we had together, maybe he will believe we can be like that again. It doesn't matter whether it's true or not. Nothing has been the same since he died, and I know that nothing ever will be, but I don't have to admit to that. No, maybe I can make Nat yearn for the days when we all went out clubbing together, or met at the pub on a Friday night. Even the holiday in Cornwall was a wonderful, beautiful memory, and Nat was present for that too. Yes, today I am going to immerse us in the past and I only hope it does not backfire on me, as I have another tactic too.

I wait as long as I can before getting up. I know he will be watching me and it is so, so tiring, being careful about everything I do, wondering what interpretation he will give my every action. If I have one cup of coffee, will he think I don't like it enough to have two? I can't have toast as the bread is all gone, so I will have to eat granola with powdered milk, but will he notice my lack of enthusiasm, how I explore the bowl with my spoon to avoid the lumps of undissolved powder? Given that he comes every day, I really don't understand why he can't bring some fresh milk with him, but somehow I don't think I will mention that. I suspect that he enjoys the giving and withholding of favours and who knows what he may withhold next?

I am almost robotic in my movements today. If anyone had told me how familiar this strange routine could become, within less than a week, I would have laughed, said what nonsense! But I wash and dress – the robe over jogging bottoms and a loose top – eat, rinse my cup and bowl, place my laundry in the bag Nat has provided for me and tidy the bed, all as if I have been doing this for years. I'm sure it would have been more difficult if I hadn't spent all those months confined to the flat, but even so. This must be a good sign. It shows that I can adapt to each new circumstance as it arises, and I will be calm when Nat arrives. I will. Even though he is now so far removed from the person I thought he was, I will behave exactly as if nothing has changed. He must not realise that I have sussed him out, or the whole edifice may tumble and reveal a much more frightening reality underneath, a reality in which he has nothing to lose.

Now that I have done all that, and there is nothing else to do, the fear sets in. I have never had an operation, not even a minor one, but I imagine it must be something like this, waiting for it to happen. I am dreading the moment when I hear the click of his key in the lock, but at the same time, the anticipation is killing me. I need to get it over with, I need things to start moving before I have time to talk myself out of it again. I would love to get on my feet, to pace up and down this space, to feel my body in motion, but I know I must be still.

I lie on the bed and think about happy times. This is what I need to do, so I try to remember all the occasions we were together, having fun. As I do, there is a dull, creeping realisation that Nat was an almost constant feature of our social lives and there are far too many to remember them all. OK, he wasn't there with us in the flat, or at my place before I gave it up, but he was there pretty much the rest of the time.

I wonder why I didn't remark on it at the time? He wasn't there at the gig, but from New Year onwards he tended to arrive with Richie wherever we were going and I simply accepted it. If it made Richie happy it made me happy, and we were usually with other people anyway. I would still go out with Olga and her crowd sometimes, but being with Richie often meant being with Nat and that was fine. There was nothing about him to dislike - although Olga wouldn't agree - as he was friendly, cheerful and helpful. Often, he would volunteer to drive, so we would all bundle into his car and go out into the country to funny little pubs with skittle alleys, to places with lovely gardens in the summer or roaring fires in the winter. It's hard not to cry when I remember those times, but I will use those memories when he comes. I have to.

At last, he's here. My heart is practically jumping out of my chest and I really need to rush to the toilet, but I force myself to remain on the bed, the robe draped around me. I think there is a very small chance that I have attained the serene and passive look I am hoping for, but this is the best I can do. My eyes strain as the door opens. How will he look at me? Will I be able to read his body language? Will he still be angry?

"Good morning, Amy," he says. His features are set in a rather blank expression but at least he does not appear cross.

"Oh, Nat, I'm so glad to see you," I say, jumping off the bed and hurrying towards him. I don't know how long I'm going to be able to last without running to the toilet, but this moment is important.

"There's been a power cut, almost the whole night. It started shortly after you left, and it didn't come back on until early this morning. I've been OK, just a bit cold, but I really wished you were here!"

"There wouldn't have been anything I could do," he says, and I suspect he does not like my interpretation of events. However, he is not going to admit to being the cause of it either, so I decide to change the subject.

"I'll make us a drink," I say, as brightly as I can, and I take a couple of cups into the bathroom to fill, solving another problem at the same time.

By the time I come out, he is prowling around the room. He used to do this in my flat, and I always assumed he was checking up on my supplies, making certain I had everything I needed, but now I am not so sure. I put one of the cups in the microwave and open the little cupboard.

"Tea or coffee?"

"Coffee," he says, but nothing more. Now he is opening up the wardrobe, running his hand along the shelf at the top, pulling open the drawers. I daren't say anything, certainly nothing I would like to say, like what the hell are you doing looking in my underwear drawer? I have to maintain this act of complete submission or there will be no chance of a positive conversation later, but I am so relieved I moved my treasures last night that I almost have to stop myself smiling.

At last he sits down. I am on the bed, at once hoping and dreading that he will come and sit next to me, but he chooses the chair.

"I had a long time with my thoughts last night," I say, "with the lights being off and all that. I was thinking about all those pubs we used to go to, you know, before Richie died. Do you remember? There was that one with the garden by the canal, I loved it there. And that one with the huge fireplace and the log fire. Nat, do you think you and I could go to places like that, one day? I'd be safe with you, I'm always safe when you're around, and we deserve some fun after what we've been through, don't we?"

I'm using the word 'we' as often as I can, and I'm painting a picture. I carry on, talking about the places we could go together, becoming almost enthusiastic as I do. One part of me never wants to spend another minute with this man, but I do want to do these things again, one day, so it's not too hard to describe what it might be like. I talk about a narrowboat holiday. Wouldn't that be fun, just the two of us? We'd be perfectly safe, and we could chill out and recover together. I describe pulling up near a pretty canal-side pub on a spring day, walking along the towpath and ordering lager and sandwiches. I'm well into this now, all my drama, all my English teacher resources in play, and I can see that he is listening. I don't think he is ruling it out.

I pause for a moment. I need some kind of response, so I shift further down the bed in order to sit as close to him as possible. I take a deep breath and reach out for his hand.

"What do you think, Nat? I'm not expecting anything straight away – I know I have no right to expect anything at all – but can I hope? Can I hope that we can have some fun together away from here, when you're ready?"

"It all depends on you, Amy," he says, but he does not remove his hand. "We wouldn't be in this situation if it wasn't for your reckless behaviour."

I tell him I know that. I know it's all my fault, I know I should have listened to him right from the start, but I'm beginning to sound like a damaged soundtrack and there is a danger that I will appear insincere, so I go back to Richie.

"You know, Richie wouldn't want us to be unhappy," I say, exerting a little more pressure on his hand. "You know how he was. He wouldn't begrudge it. Just because he can't be here himself, it doesn't mean that we can't carry on without him."

This is really difficult for me, and I hate myself for saying it, even though I do not mean a single word. It is probably true, Richie would not want me to be unhappy, but he would hate Nat for what he is doing now. I'm so glad I do not believe in any form of afterlife, as I can't imagine what he would feel if he could see me now. But it has to be done. I have to say these things. I have to imply that I'm beginning to get over Richie and that maybe Nat could take his place. I'm not pushing the physical side of things as even the thought of it makes me sick, but the idea of two mates out and about, one caring and protective and the other eternally grateful and submissive, is something that I think he is beginning to like.

I think that is enough for now. I need to let the notion settle in his mind for a while. Maybe he will like it better the more he thinks about it. I have done the best job I could and called upon all my powers of description and persuasion, so I gently remove my hand and talk about lunch.

Fortunately, it appears that Nat has forgiven me for my ingratitude where food is concerned and he has brought more supplies in his sports bag. There is a sliced loaf for the freezer, but also some lovely rustic rolls in a variety of flavours – one with cheese, one with walnuts, one with olives – and we eat these with rich camembert and a herby cream cheese.

"This is almost like being abroad," I joke, and my heart leaps, as there is a little smile on his lips.

"Maybe that could be arranged," he says.

I can hardly believe my luck. He really does want me in his life, and he is clearly vulnerable to this kind of tactic. I have to think fast. I was not expecting to achieve this much in such a short space of time and my plans are only sketchy. What should I do next? There is only one thing for it. I will have to play my final card, so I get up and stack the plates. He's on the bed this time, so I sit next to him. Close, but not too close. Friendly, companionable, devoted even. I don't care any more, this is my opportunity and I have to exploit it.

"I had a dream last night," I say. He doesn't reply, but he is listening. "We are walking on a cliff, you, me and Richie, and it isn't very safe. The edge is unstable but we have to do it, I don't know why. You know how it is with dreams. Anyway, just as we are nearly there, a big chunk of cliff starts to crack and it's about to fall into the sea, taking Richie with it, but you grab him by the arm and pull him up, even though it nearly takes you down too, and I love you so much for saving him. It ended there, the dream, but it is so true Nat. I know you would have given your life for Richie if you could have, and I think my dream was telling me that I must trust you, whatever happens."

I don't know what I was expecting, but it certainly wasn't this. There is a silence, but I know something is going to happen as I see his hands clench into fists. When he speaks, his words are cold enough to frost the inside of the window, if it wasn't frosted already.

"For fuck's sake, Amy. Will you stop going on about fucking Richie?"

I can't get my head around this and I'm not really thinking about my reply. I didn't have much of a script in the first place, but it's abandoned now, that's for sure.

"What's wrong, Nat?" I cry. "I thought you would like to remember him. I know I do. He was your best friend ..."

"Yeah, yeah. The best friend a man could ever have. I know. I wrote the eulogy, remember? But it wasn't as simple as that, Amy. If you'd known him longer you would have seen how selfish he was, how he always wanted everything for himself. He wasn't the saint everyone thought he was, believe me."

I can't stand this. I'm way beyond being able to control myself now, so I tell him that's a terrible thing to say, tell him how much Richie cared for him and how lovely he was. But Nat is on his feet, and he is marching up and down the room, twisting his hands together, his face contorted.

"Amy, will you shut up?" he shouts. "I'm sick to fucking death of it. Richie, Richie, Richie! Everyone loved poor old Richie, didn't they? You don't have a clue what I had to do to support him, how many times I bailed him out, how many times I sorted out the messes he got himself into. He was a weak, ungrateful parasite, and he had it coming to him!"

Now there is a silence beyond all silences. Nat has turned away from me and I have become very cold. Prickles are creeping across the back of my neck and down my spine and Nat's words are bouncing around the room like a soundless echo. He had it coming to him. What did that mean? He turns back to me, white-faced.

"Look, don't take any notice of me," he says. "It's getting on top of me, all this. You're right. We have spent far too much time cooped up. It's time we had a holiday.

I'm going to go now, but when I come back tomorrow I'll bring some brochures with me, or I'll bookmark some websites."

Somehow, I manage a smile. My voice, when I reply, sounds thin and reedy, as if it has been electronically modified. I don't know what I'm saying, not really, as it's coming from some automatic system somewhere in my brain, some ancient form of self-protection, left over from when we lived in trees and danger came from all sides. There is only one danger in my life, but now I know exactly what a terrible, serious danger it is.

He's gone now, and I need to cry. More than that, I need to scream and howl. I need to rage and throw myself on the bed, beating the pillows. I need to imagine Nat is there and I am pummelling him into oblivion, for now I know it all. The one thing that never, ever occurred to me. It was Nat who killed Richie, wasn't it? He didn't say it as such, but I could tell by his face. It was Nat who hung around outside the flat with a sharpened kitchen knife and plunged it into Richie's heart. It was Nat who walked away and left him bleeding. It was Nat who didn't call for an ambulance or any kind of help, as he wanted him dead. After all, he had it coming.

But I can't scream and I can't rage. I go into the bathroom and cry for as long as I think I can get away with it, but the rest will have to wait. I am now remarkably calm, remarkably in control as I lie on the bed and wonder how it unfolded. I know from the inquest that Richie was attacked from the left hand side. Did he know it was Nat? Was there a brief moment of pleasure at seeing his friend – oh, hello mate! What are you doing here? Then the terrible realisation that the man he would have trusted with his life was actually about to take it? Or was it all too quick for recognition? I hope so. I hope Richie didn't have to die knowing that his best friend secretly hated him, envied him his popularity, his friends, his girlfriend.

I can see it now. This is nothing to do with keeping me safe. This is all about possession. I belonged to Richie – as

Nat would have seen it – and he wanted me for himself. I expect he could cope all the time he was included in our plans, and maybe he thought that he only needed to bide his time and I would realise he was a better choice, but Richie was going to take me away, to somewhere so far from him that even a visit would be difficult. He wouldn't see me for a year and all his work would be in vain. He couldn't let that happen and he didn't. Nobody would ever know, nobody would ever guess.

It's later now, and it's getting dark but I have left all the lights off. I'm past caring what he thinks about that, as I need to concentrate. I cannot eat, or drink, or sleep until I have finished working this out. This is a new situation and it calls for a different response. Strangely, I'm not even scared.

December 29th

Today, I am made of steel. I may look the same on the outside, pale and insubstantial, becoming increasingly like one of those colourless and semi-transparent creatures that live in caves where the light never penetrates, but inside I have changed. Bitterness and rage have transformed me, so now I am untouchable, unstoppable. I have a core as impenetrable as the wood of that door and he will find this out when he comes.

Not immediately though. First, I have to prepare him, so I feign sleep until it has been light for a while, just in case he is still in bed and misses my performance, then I get up and go to the bathroom. I shower – after a fashion, I still hate it – but all I need is to be wet, then I dry myself a little and put on only a pair of pants and the robe. I stand behind the door for a few seconds, taking a few deep breaths, then out I go, on stage. My robe is tied only loosely – why would I need to cover up, no-one is here to watch me? – and I let it slip open to the waist as I drift around making tea, defrosting bread, reaching up to the toaster.

There's more of this, much more, as I eat and clear away, and then maybe I'm a little chilly, so I slip off the robe and wriggle into a bra and a tight top, but I love that robe, don't I? I love it so much that I want to feel it on my skin, so, no jeans or jogging bottoms for me today. I don't bother tying it, but let it flow around me, behind me, as I find excuses to move around the room. Now, that's a good idea! I'll tidy up my clothes, starting with the underwear, so I get it all out and put it in piles on the bed, which necessitates a good deal of holding it up for inspection, of wandering back and forth, then I have to put it back, with a lot more bending. At one point, I even sit cross-legged on the floor with the robe spread out around me, hoping I'm facing at least one camera as I fold T-shirts. There's no stopping me today, and I put jeans, socks and another top on a shelf so they are ready when I need them.

I have other preparations. I carry them out too, but they are off-camera. All is ready. All I need now is for Nat to come, and I hope he has been watching my little performance. If he hasn't, if he has decided to go to work without even looking at me, all this will have been in vain, but somehow I can't see it. He will want to find out how I am reacting to his blunder, if I am throwing myself around with grief and anger, or hiding away like a little mouse. That is not what he will have seen. He will have seen things today that he has not seen before and I only hope it is enough.

Sure enough, he is here early today. I knew he would not be able to keep away, but I pull the robe around me and tie it as I hear the lock turn. After all, I am very modest when I am not alone. He looks apprehensive as he enters and he comes in one bit at a time, head round the door as if to check all is well, then an arm and a leg and a hesitant smile. I, of course, am delighted to see him. I have completely forgotten about any throwaway comment he may have made yesterday. Oh yes, it is banished from my mind and I only want to concentrate on that holiday.

"Did you bring the brochures?" I ask, a note of excitement in my voice.

"No, sorry, I haven't had time to go to any travel agents, but I have my tablet."

I can't believe there is wi-fi here. It seems like such a strange anachronism, when I have spent a week in this room without even a radio, let alone a computer, but I keep that thought to myself and get up to make a drink. It is amazing how difficult to manage silk can be, and I am having a lot of trouble keeping the robe from slipping open today, especially as I approach him with two cups of coffee. I sit down beside him on the bed, put our coffees on the floor beside us and make a half-hearted attempt to cover my legs. I need to sit quite close as it is only a small tablet and how will I be able to read the descriptions otherwise?

This is going very well. Nat is happy, I can tell. He has lost that prickly feeling he's had a lot recently and I can concentrate on what I have to do without worrying too much about his mood.

"Look at that one!" I say, reaching across to point out a lovely apartment with a balcony overlooking a pool. "I can see us sitting there, can't you? A couple of cocktails, you in your shorts, me in a bikini. It would be so lovely to feel the sun on my skin again."

Nat scrolls through more pictures of the apartment. I gasp at the sumptuous shower room, murmur approval at the neat little fitted kitchen.

"Ah, it wouldn't do," he says, when the bedroom appears. "No twin beds." I decide that now is probably as good a time as any.

"Would that be a problem?" I ask, with what I hope is a hint of a raised eyebrow.

"Well, I just thought …"

"What did you think, Nat? Did you think I want to live like a nun for the rest of my life? Did you think that I would ever consider a relationship with anyone else, after all you have done for me? There's no point in either of us spending the rest of our lives single and unhappy, is there?"

There is a silence. I think I may have blown it, that he may explode any minute and start calling me a whore and all the other horrible things he said in those letters, but he is not angry, he is taking it in.

"I thought that Richie …"

I can't allow Richie to come in and change the mood now, so I place a finger on Nat's lips. I feel a bit sick, but he would never be able to tell.

"Like I said yesterday, Richie would not want either of us to be lonely, and if the two people he loved best can make each other happy, well I think he would approve. We can't live in the past, Nat. We're both too young for that. Why don't we see what the future can offer us?"

God, I'm good. I am even better than I thought I would be. I take my hand away and look at his mouth as if I'm expecting my finger to have left an impression there. Maybe it did.

"I don't know what to say," he says.

"Well, in my experience, when you don't know what to say, it's best to see what you can do," I reply. There is a stone where my heart used to be. I had to put it there last night, or this wouldn't have worked, but I hope it holds out. I take the tablet and put it on the floor, then I take his hand and pull it across so it is resting on my thigh, on the silk. My stone heart is beating fit to bust and I have a roaring in my ears, but I'm acting. Hang on to that, I tell myself. This isn't real. This isn't you. This is the Amy who has been sent to save you and you have to let her do her work.

It isn't long before he has moved closer and pulled me to him for a kiss. I knew this would happen, it is part of the plan, but it is worse than I thought. This is what he wanted to do in Cornwall, that evening we were alone and a little drunk, and I let him hug me because that song had made me cry. Him too. I had only let it continue for a few seconds as it didn't feel right, but now I have to respond. I have to act as if I am enjoying it. As his tongue begins to explore mine and his breathing increases, I seriously think I am going to be sick, so I pull away gently.

"Wow," I say, breathily. "Actions do speak louder than words, don't they?"

I can see that I have him now. The evidence for that is pushing against his chinos for all to see, so I allow my eyes to drop, then look back up at him. I undo the robe and wriggle backwards so I am sitting on the bed with my back to my pillow. He turns to look at me.

"Are you going to join me?" I say.

Nat does not move. Conflicting emotions sweep across his features. This has all happened very quickly and he is suspicious. I would be, in his place, however much I wanted it to be true. Have I blown it?

"Nat, do you remember Cornwall?" I say.

He does not reply, but his eyes catch mine. I move across the bed so I am behind him and I start to hum. 'Street Spirit', that lilting refrain, quietly, gently, inches from his ear. I place two fingers on the back of his neck and run them up and down slowly, in time with the song. Then I stop.

"Do you remember that night? We were talking and 'Street Spirit' came on. It made me cry – you must remember Nat, I could see it meant something to you too. And you hugged me – we hugged each other. We connected that night, didn't we? Being here together is making me remember that. It's making me think."

I start to hum again. My fingers are back on his neck. I move a little closer.

"What is it making you think?" he asks. His voice is husky and he has to clear his throat.

"Can't you guess?"

"I'd like you to tell me," he says. He is leaning backwards.

I put my hands on his shoulders and whisper in his ear. "It's making me think I've been given a second chance. I thought my life was over, but I'm beginning to see a future. It's all about being safe Nat – that's always what I'm looking for – and you've given me that. You've given me hope."

A bit more humming in his ear, a few words of the lyrics, a little breathless sigh, a tongue that just happens to brush his earlobe and he's kissing me again. We fall back against the pillows. My robe is a sex toy, I can tell he loves the feel of it, so I let my hand wander down to the bulge which is now straining against his buttons and I undo them, one by one. My hand creeps around, teasing him, and now I have one leg over him. But then I stop, sit up.

"What's wrong?" he says, his mouth wet and blurry.

"Nothing," I say, "apart from these chinos getting in

the way." I make a point of taking them off slowly, insisting he lies there still. I return to keep the fires burning with a little stroke, a little pressure, a teasing little kiss on the thigh, until I have his trousers off and I have put them on the chair. I return to him, lie next to him then slowly work my way over until I am astride him, moving up and down for a while, then nuzzling his neck and lying not quite still, then doing the whole routine again. I undo the buttons of his shirt and run my tongue over his nipples. Now he is practically crazy for it, and one hand creeps down and starts to fumble with his pants, with mine, so I know the time has come.

I start to make some little moans. I whisper his name, I talk dirty to him. I put my tongue in his ear, and my hand under the pillow and I find it. I hold it tight, then I raise myself, hands either side of his head, as if this is the moment, this is the moment he has been waiting for, then I lift my hand and I strike. It is the moment I have been waiting for, and he doesn't scream or shout, only makes a little grunt of surprise.

"That's for Richie!"

There is a mini-screwdriver sticking out of his chest and a little trickle of blood running down to his armpit. But it's not where I intended it to be. It is nowhere near his heart, and I scramble to get off him as I know I have no time. In my haste, my knee catches his groin and I wish I'd thought of that, I wish I'd done it properly, as now he's doubled up and groaning.

"You fucking bitch! You fucking lying bitch."

But I have no time to waste. I have no time to tell him how much I hate him, how much I wish he was dead. I pick up his trousers and shake them, grab the keys and hurl myself towards the door. My hands are quivering so much I can barely fit the key in the lock, but I do it, turning back to see what is happening on the bed. He is still hunched up so I can't see whether he is bleeding much or not. I'm through the door and down the steep steps in seconds. There's no time for the clothes I had placed in the wardrobe, no time for shoes. I don't even care that my robe is open and I am half-naked underneath. I don't even take the keys.

Now I am at the bottom of the second flight of stairs. There is Flat A and there is the front door. I am only six feet from freedom, and I nearly skid on all the junk mail that has accumulated in the hall as I rush to the door. It is a Yale lock but it won't turn. Why won't it turn? I shake it, I rattle it, but then I see that there is a lock on the inside too. Nat has thought of everything and now it is all slipping away. I can't be this close to freedom and not achieve it, so I turn to look at the hallway but there is nothing. Just the one door, Flat A, the faded wallpaper, the mosaic-tiled floor and the heap of mail stacked in a corner and spread around by the door.

That's when I hear him.

"Amy."

He's on the stairs, and he's saying my name. He is not shouting, he is not crying, but he is getting closer.

I fly to the front door again, beat my fists on the stained glass panels, scream and cry. "Help! Help! Somebody help me, please!"

But it's pointless. He is walking down the stairs to me. He is wearing his trousers now, but no shirt, and there is a small hole where the screwdriver was. Blood trickles down his chest but he seems oblivious to this. He is slow, he is quiet, he is calm.

"Ah, there you are," he says. "Are you going to be sensible and come back upstairs with me or am I going to have to take you?"

He sounds like my mother. There is no point in resisting, any more than there was resisting her, and I am scared by his blankness. He looks like a computer-generated image, with dull eyes and thin, tight lips. I know when I'm beaten if I know nothing else, so I edge around him and walk back to the stairs, keeping him in my sight.

"Up you go." His voice is very flat and I'm trying to work out how to deal with this as he continues to speak.

"I can't believe I've been so stupid. How could I let myself be tricked by a cheating little bitch like this? After all the times she's lied to me, let me down, thrown my kindness back in my face! But that's women for you, isn't it? They always do it. Well, this is the last time. No fucking bitch is going to get inside my head again, especially not this one."

There's more. I'm climbing the stairs sideways, like a crab, as slowly as I can, trying to block out what he's saying, trying to think of something, anything I can do. I daren't look away from him but I'm terrified to catch those dead eyes. Every step seems to take a lifetime and he has really lost it now, winding himself up, tormenting himself. We reach the top of the first flight and he prods me in the side so I start to climb the second flight.

"The problem is, I'm not sure if I can leave her alone now," he mutters, pausing as if the act of thought is too hard to execute whilst climbing such a steep staircase. "Who knows what she will do next? Shall I tie her up? That would keep her out of trouble, but then how long could I leave her? How would she eat and drink? What about the toilet?"

I'm beginning to really panic now. There are only a few more steps and we'll be at the top. What if he ties me up in there and doesn't come back? It won't take me weeks to die, it will be days. Suddenly, my semi-comfortable existence in that room seems safe and predictable and I almost wish I could have it back. I contemplate saying something, but his anger is almost palpable. It is burning a hole in my heart and I daren't say a word to him as I don't know what it might provoke. Now he is moving again and I have to shuffle on, almost crawling up the last few steps on my bottom, like a little child.

So now we are at the top of the stairs, crammed together on the tiny landing. Any minute now, he will reach around me or move me to one side, the door will open and then what? My heart is pounding like a steamhammer and I am clammy with fear. But what's that?

There is a noise coming from below. A thumping sound, like someone banging on the door. It is someone banging on the door and my heart leaps. He turns around and I don't even think about it. I put both my hands on his back and push as hard as I can.

He can't stop himself. There's only one banister and he doesn't grab it in time. The stairs are steep and he tumbles down head first, head over heels, and crashes to a heap at the bottom. I don't even wait to see if he moves, but I'm down those stairs faster than I've ever moved in my whole life. I'm like a gazelle as I leap over his still and twisted body, then I'm down the second flight and at the door screaming.

"I'm here! Help me! Help me! I can't get out and he's here. I think he will kill me!"

It takes ages for the police to break down the door. They ask me if I can get the key but I can't. I'm sitting by the door to Flat A, my arms around my knees, and I'm shaking so much I can't walk another foot, let alone up the stairs to frisk a madman for his keys.

They help me up, they help me out. There is a nice policewoman and there is Olga. They take one arm each and there is the street. It's a dull, drizzly day, the sky is grey, the pavement is wet, the houses are hunkered down against the cold, but this is the most wonderful, the most beautiful sight I have ever seen. I will never forget this moment, as I step out wearing nothing but a silk gown. I will never forget the smell of traffic and the chill of the air, for I am free.

Six months later

It's hard to believe that I'm here again. The pounding in my chest, the butterflies in my stomach. After all that has happened in the past few months, can this really be true? But yes, it is. Despite everything.

There is no Nat to bother me now, that isn't the problem. "Mad as a hatter," says Olga, when she talks about him. She's quite proud of the fact that she was the only one to see through him and yes, he is completely mad. Not that they used that terminology when they decided that he wasn't fit to stand trial. Nat is a sociopath – which is apparently not quite the same as a psychopath but with many of the same characteristics – but he is high-functioning. Quite possibly, he would have carried on leading a relatively normal life if Richie hadn't asked him to help sort Greg out. For some reason, he became fixated on me and looking after me. It gave him a buzz, and then that grew until he wasn't happy unless he could have me all to himself and keep me safe all the time. That was when all his powers of manipulation came into play. I shouldn't blame myself, they tell me. That's what they are good at, people like Nat, and there wasn't anything I could have done. There are even days when I can believe that, from time to time.

We will probably never know for sure if he killed Richie. He denies it – when he is fit enough to deny anything – but there is no evidence either way and there will never be any charges unless he gets better one day and admits it. I don't know what to think. Some days I remember his face when he said Richie had it coming to him and I'm certain he did it, but sometimes I'm not so sure. Maybe it was just a random act, and Nat thought there was a kind of poetic justice in that. I suppose it doesn't matter really, as Richie is dead and nothing will ever bring him back whether or not I find out the truth.

Olga says that being a sociopath, high-functioning or not, shouldn't be an excuse. She thinks he should stand trial anyway, but actually it's his psychosis that is keeping him in a secure ward at present and she knows that really. She also says it's a pity I didn't finish him off, but I'm glad he didn't die. I know I had enough of an excuse and I doubt very much I would have gone to trial, but I would have to live with it forever. Strangely, I don't even hate him any more. Why waste time and energy hating someone like that?

Of course I'm more grateful to Olga than I can ever express. If our friendship was ever in any doubt, it certainly won't be again. Her suspicions were aroused when she saw posts on Facebook, apparently from me. These described my trip to Scotland, and said what a lovely hotel Nat had found for me and how much I was looking forward to him joining me for New Year. There were photographs of the hotel and one of me wrapped up in a warm coat and woolly hat, standing by a stretch of water. All this appeared to be fine at first, and she was glad that I seemed to have got away from Nat for a few days if nothing else, so she sent me our usual little coded message: What's the scenery like, chick?

My reply was a post about how I could see mountains in the distance and a loch from my bedroom window, and that's when Olga knew for certain that something was wrong. I would have known, just as she did, what that question really meant and it was nothing to do with mountains or lochs, so she hurried round to my flat. When she got there, she found Nat just leaving, so she questioned him about my trip, asked for the name of the hotel and where it was, but he refused to tell her. He said it had to be kept a secret because of Greg, but she didn't believe a word of it and went straight to the police.

She still likes to tell the story sometimes. Although I was obviously in a much worse state, it was traumatic for her too, and she's never been one for bottling things up. So we sit there in our new flat on her big squashy sofa, just like I had dreamed we would do, and she tells me how difficult it was to persuade the police. She describes the agony of waiting for the authorities in London to track down a property in Nat's name and laughs when she describes how she remembered about Nat's inheritance.

"Do you remember?" she says. "You told me about his aunt leaving him a house, and I said maybe I could like him better after all. Maybe a house in London could make him quite attractive!"

I laugh along with her, but I don't remember that conversation. There's a lot I either don't remember or don't choose to, and I certainly don't want to spend hours recounting what happened in that room. Being in an almost permanent state of shock for so many days has its effect on you, but Olga understands and we confine our reminiscences to my rescue. This is something that is likely to achieve legendary status the way things are going, but that's fine. It's perfectly fine by me.

So, it's not Nat, and of course it's not Greg who is causing my butterflies. I went to apologise to him and his parents, not that long ago, and they were amazing. They knew all about it and they completely understood how I had been tricked. Greg is still with the same girlfriend and has put any thoughts of me out of his mind, but he still likes his music and he still comes to gigs. Maybe I will see him tonight.

The room is filling up now and I'm sitting at that same table, my guts churning away, wondering if I'm doing the right thing. But it's too late to change my mind now, as Anton is at the mic.

"And now, please welcome Amy Barker. She's been away for a while, but we're delighted to have her back!"

I walk across the floor and take the couple of steps up to the stage. I stand behind the mic. The lights are in my eyes, but Olga is there beside me and she gives me a smile as we link arms and the intro starts. For a moment, I think I've lost it, that my voice will never return, but then I imagine Richie is there watching me and I know I'll be alright. I can do it. I really wish he could be there in the audience, smiling that proud smile of his, I wish it so much, but he can't be, so this one's for him.

I'm only singing the chorus – one step at a time, after all – but, when it comes, Olga and I belt it out together, just like we used to, just like we will do again.

It's 'Girls Just Want To Have Fun', but it wouldn't matter what it was, because the audience is joining in, everyone is smiling and dancing and I think yes, it's OK. I really am going to be fine after all.

The End

Printed in Great Britain
by Amazon.co.uk, Ltd.,
Marston Gate.